He took her h_____ __ _____ _____d
even in her p___ _____ ____ a
sh_ver of react___ _____ _____n
h_ before looki___

'_ __k…' he finally said. 'I haven't the faintest clue
h___ to tell you this, but the clinic said they would
c___act you and as far as I can see that would be a
d___ster. Maybe it's a disaster anyway, but at least
n__ you'll see exactly what's happened. You deserve
t_ _now and I need to tell you.'

H_ wasn't making any sense but he did seem
g__uinely concerned—which, together with his talk
o_ __e clinic, had the nerves in Joey's tummy heading
s___ight for riot mode.

'_ __haps you could just blurt it out?' she suggested as
t__ _ension in the air between them reached seismic
p__portions.

_ *blurt it out? That's rich!* Max thought to himself.
*__e's this stunning woman, ready to pop any minute,
___ a total stranger walks in…*

'__ thing is,' he said, as thoughts of the baby
___nded him of his mission. *And* of the mess they
__ _e in!

'__ thing is…?' she prompted—reasonably gently,
___sidering his eruption into her life and the tension
sne must be feeling. To make matters worse, she then
turned ___ ards him and reached out to rest one hand
on his.

'Oh, the_____s
hand so_____e
having r_

Dear Reader

In the early stages of writing this book I met a remarkable woman—Alison Ray. Alison isn't a multi-millionaire philanthropist, or a corporation with money to give away, but on a trip to Africa she saw a need—and from a smallish town in central Queensland, on the edge of the Outback, she set out to do something about it.

When Alison spoke to me of Chainda, a settlement outside Lusaka in Zambia with 26,000 inhabitants, seven thousand of whom are orphans or other vulnerable children, I realised for the first time just how devastating the Aids epidemic was. Seven thousand orphans, or children whose grandparents or other carers are becoming too old or sick or frail to care for them... The number staggered me. So did Alison's drive and tenacity.

She began small, raising money locally, then found a group of helpers willing to form a committee and from there registered a charity, calling it Our Rainbow House, because eventually what the group hopes to do is provide a safe haven for at least some of these children. Already the group has done a lot with their early programmes, and now has a teacher and a small school for forty-four of the children. But there is so much more left to do. You can read about the organisation, the settlement and the children on www.ourrainbowhouse.org.au and follow them on Facebook. I'm sure you'll be as inspired as I was by this very special woman.

There *is* a programme underway to vaccinate healthy young men and women in an attempt to halt the spread of Aids in Africa, but this is happening in Uganda and Kenya, so in this book—right near the end—I sent Max off to Zambia to do it there. Writers are allowed to make things up!

All the best

Meredith

THE ACCIDENTAL DADDY

BY
MEREDITH WEBBER

Published in Great Britain 2014
by Mills & Boon, an imprint of Harlequin (UK) Limited,
Eton House, 18-24 Paradise Road, Richmond, Surrey, TW9 1SR

© 2014 Meredith Webber

ISBN: 978 0 263 90777 3

Harlequin (UK) Limited's policy is to use papers that are natural,
renewable and recyclable products and made from wood grown in
sustainable forests. The logging and manufacturing processes conform
to the legal environmental regulations of the country of origin.

Printed and bound in Spain
by Blackprint CPI, Barcelona

Meredith Webber says of herself, 'Once I read an article which suggested that Mills & Boon® were looking for new Medical Romance™ authors. I had one of those "I can do that" moments, and gave it a try. What began as a challenge has become an obsession—though I do temper the "butt on seat" career of writing with dirty but healthy outdoor pursuits, fossicking through the Australian Outback in search of gold or opals. Having had some success in all of these endeavours, I now consider I've found the perfect lifestyle.'

Recent titles by Meredith Webber:

DATE WITH A SURGEON PRINCE
ONE BABY STEP AT A TIME
CHRISTMAS WHERE SHE BELONGS
THE SHEIKH AND THE SURROGATE MUM
NEW DOC IN TOWN*
ORPHAN UNDER THE CHRISTMAS TREE*
MELTING THE ARGENTINE DOCTOR'S HEART
TAMING DR TEMPEST

Christmas at Crystal Cove

These books are also available in eBook format from www.millsandboon.co.uk

Dedication

With many thanks to the incomparable Marion Lennox,
without whose advice and encouragement this book
would never have been finished.

CHAPTER ONE

'You might already be a father!'

Shock held Max Winthrop rooted to his chair, staring at his friend and fellow doctor in total disbelief.

Less than thirty minutes ago he'd stood outside the IVF clinic, trying to work out how he felt.

Uncertain?

Angsty?

Heaven help him, was there even such a word?

Get on with it, he'd told himself. *You've made the decision, now walk in there and see Pete.*

But there he'd stood, his mind flashing back seven years…

Seven years ago, filled with determination to beat a recently diagnosed cancer, he'd left something of himself here—a deposit for the future.

Back then it had been Step One of his 'positive action' programme, coming right before Step Two—Begin Aggressive Treatment.

Step Three had been Finish Treatment, followed closely by Step Four, Climb Mount Everest.

It hadn't been a bad plan for a bloke in his mid-twenties who'd suddenly discovered he had an aggressive form of non-Hodgkin lymphoma, and although his then fiancée had muttered a few doubts about Step Four on the plan, she'd agreed that he needed something special in the way of a goal.

He suspected Get Married had been her choice for 'something special,' although it had never been put into words.

Now, two fiancées and some serious life changes later, he'd decided the time had come to have his frozen sperm destroyed.

'Why now?' his friend Pete had asked when Max had finally made it in through the door.

Seven years ago Max had decided to use this particular facility because his friend Pete was working in the clinic.

Pete was now one of the co-owners, and a good part of the reason the clinic had become extremely successful in the competitive world of assisted pregnancies.

'Why now?' Pete asked again.

'You should know that,' Max finally answered. 'You're the one who told me it loses its motility the longer it's kept frozen.'

'So you've had a test and your little swimmers are okay?' Pete probed.

'Not exactly,' he replied, 'but if I do happen to find a woman who'll have me, then I'll tell her the risks and we'll take our chances.'

'Get tested first. I can do it here and now. Or get it done.'

'Thanks, but no thanks,' Max said firmly. It made no difference now. Regardless, he wouldn't be taking changes with long-frozen sperm. Besides, he'd spent the last few months debating this in his head, weighing up the pros and cons of future marriage, accepting, finally, that the women in his life were probably right. He *wasn't* good marriage material.

Or family material.

Father material...

This last bit of the argument was the strongest, coming as it did from his own memories—the memory of the child he'd been when his adored father had left the family. It had been the final weight added to the 'con' side—the catalyst for this final decision. At times he still felt the pain of that time—and to inflict that on another child?

His child?

Maybe he wasn't sure. Maybe that was why he'd rushed into preserving sperm before treatment all those years ago, but the years had made him even less certain he could cope with fatherhood. This final act was simply admitting it.

'I've made the decision, Pete,' Max added. 'I want it destroyed.'

Pete shrugged, woken the laptop on his desk from its sleep and begun typing, sending a message to a printer somewhere in the bowels of the building.

He then used his phone to summon a lackey—a very attractive female lackey.

'Jess, would you make sure someone in the cryo room gets the details on that printout I just sent through; then rustle up some coffee? Preferences, Max?'

Max gave his coffee order, then watched the delectable Jess leave the room.

'Eyes off, old man,' Pete said to him. 'She's engaged to one of our new staff members—a genius who's going to make this company famous worldwide. Although...'

He paused, studying Max as if he were a newly inseminated egg.

'Again, I have to ask, are you sure about this decision?'

Max had to laugh.

'Just because I've decided marriage and children aren't for me, it doesn't mean I've become a monk. You're a happily married man so you've no idea how many intelligent, attractive women there are out there who feel just as I do. They've decided, carefully and rationally, that marriage isn't for them, but they're happy to have no-strings relationships with men who feel the same.'

Pete nodded.

'Not surprised at all,' he said. 'We've a couple of them working here. Women who love their work, enjoy their leisure time in all manner of ways and just don't see marriage or kids as an imperative in their lives.'

Jess returned with the two coffees and a plate of wafer-thin almond biscotti. She put the tray on table by the window, assured Pete someone was working on his request and departed once again.

Max picked up his coffee, while Pete studied a message that had obviously come through on his mobile.

'Drink your coffee, I'll be back in a minute,' he said, as he headed out the door.

Watching him go, Max knew he'd made the right career decision. Not for him this office life, running a successful company but always being called in to solve this or check that. Working in a hospital was much the same, noisy pagers summoning him from one place to another. Private practice might be okay, but it had changed—less personal in so many ways.

So the lecturing he did, combined with research on the spread of infection in developing countries, plus hands-on work in the same area, was *his* career choice. It also gave him freedom to head off and climb the odd mountain when he needed to clear his head. He had no strings attached and it worked for him.

Another confirmation this was also the right decision.

Until Pete strode back into the room, obviously flustered, clutching a small metal container not unlike a miniature silver flask and a sheaf of paperwork.

And delivered the blow that had Max stuck in his chair.

'Max…mate, I don't know how to tell you this. This is unbelievable. Unbelievable that it's happened, and that it's happened to you. Max…I just need to say it. You might already be a father.'

Aware that he was probably doing a very good impression of a stunned mullet, Max could only stare at his friend.

Finally he got it out. 'What the hell are you talking about?'

'There's a mistake with the cross-match,' Pete croaked.

'You want to explain?'

Max heard his voice as if it came from someone else. Icy cold. Controlled. Not his.

'The cross-match... Names matched to codes, verified every step of the way. But your name has the wrong code on it. They've checked and there's a matching mistake. Your code with another name on it. But, hell, Max, yours has been used.'

'My sperm has been used?'

'That's what I've been trying to say. It might even be a mistake—it has to be a mistake—though how it happened, I have no idea. But it's been used. There's a pregnancy.'

Could a life change so completely so quickly?

He stared at his friend. Pete stared back in consternation, then stood and walked to the window. He barked into his phone, demanding more information.

Max stared at his back, then down to the folder on the desk. He flicked it open.

A name...details...

Pete turned, saw what he was looking at and snatched the file away.

They stared at each other.

Shock eased and words came. Demands. Anger

He rose to his feet, coffee forgotten as he tried to absorb this impossible news. Icy anger.

'There's b-been a m-mix-up,' Pete stammered. 'Honestly, Max, this never happens—the checks and balances... I'll find out how and why, but right now—'

'You're saying someone's having my baby! Who?'

'I can't tell you that—it's bad enough it's happened. I mean, we'll have to tell the woman when we sort out just what's happened. God, this could ruin us!'

'Ruin you? Ruin the clinic? What about me?'

'And the poor woman who thinks she's having her dead husband's baby...'

Anger had him pacing—back and forth in front of the desk. But... Dead husband. The two words that brought Max to a halt, to loom over the desk once again.

'What do you mean, dead husband?'

Pete looked up at him, his face pale and haggard.

'Her husband died shortly after he was here, and she finally decided to use the sperm—have his child.'

'The fact remains she's having *my* baby,' Max growled. He raked his hair. 'Hell. Do we...?' He was struggling to get his head around it. 'Do I need to know? Does *she* need to know?'

'There's no way we can do that,' said Pete. 'The DNA... it's yours, not his. That has so many implications...'

It did. Implications were all he was seeing right now, and he didn't like any of them.

'I need to meet her,' he said at last, trying to think logically. 'I need to speak to her. How far gone is she? Is the pregnancy viable?' So many questions...

Pete recovered enough to straighten in his seat, colour returning to his face.

'Max, you need to leave this to us. We'll sort it. Somehow. This business is all about confidentiality. I'll see her, I'll explain—keep you right out of it.'

'Keep me right out of it when it's my baby you're talking about?' He couldn't get his head around the words. *My baby.*

This didn't make sense. Why the surge of certainty? Why the instant knowledge that if this was his baby, he wanted to be involved?

Maybe the rational decision he'd walked in here with hadn't been so rational after all.

And he'd seen the file.

'It's Joanne McMillan,' he said, watching his friend's face. 'Dr Joanne McMillan.'

'You can't know.' Pete clutched his file in horror, his colour fading even further. 'You shouldn't have seen. Forget it. We need to talk to her—explain. *I* need to see her, not you.'

'Oh, no! There is no way some woman is going to have my baby without my at least meeting her—checking her out.'

'But it won't be your baby—don't you see that?' Pete held out his hands in a plea to his friend. 'You've told me you don't want children. You've made a rational and reasoned decision about it and come in to have your sperm destroyed. The best way to treat it is to consider you made an anonymous donation.'

'No way!' He hardly knew what he was saying; he only knew it was a basic, instinctive truth. 'This is my baby— and while I might not want it, at least I need to see it's going to a good home. I do have *some* responsibility. I should have *some* say in the matter. As she'll want to know—want to check me out surely.'

Light-bulb moment!

'You said you'd go and see her to explain. Why don't you let me go? You can make an appointment for someone from the clinic who needs to see her and I'll go.'

'And do what?' Pete demanded.

'I'll work that out when we meet. I imagine she's going to be so shocked to learn what's happened she's not really going to care who the father is, not right away. And if she's happy to go along with the anonymous donor thing and I decide she'll do as a mother, then, okay, I won't tell her.'

'Of course she'll do as a mother—she's a doctor, a paediatrician, in fact. She'll make an excellent mother.'

'You have *got* to be joking!' Max muttered. His mind was heading off on all sorts of tangents. How could he feel protective of…his sperm? A stranger's pregnancy? All he knew was that he was.

'You and I both remember men and women from our university days who would make appalling parents,' he told Pete. He was sounding a lot less flustered than Pete right now, more in control. 'Medical training doesn't include extensive courses on good parenting, and even if it did, it wouldn't have got through to people like Mike Wills, whose eyes were on the dollar signs right from the start, or that daffy woman who was always forgetting her handbag or her lecture notes and kept losing her car in the car park. Can you imagine how she'd be with kids? "Now, did I have two or three of them when I left home?" she'll be saying.'

He was talking drivel, but it was helping him back towards a semblance of normality. It was strengthening his determination to meet the woman who would be the mother of the child he hadn't wanted to have.

'How far along is the pregnancy?' he demanded, and then, as Pete didn't answer, he grabbed the file and flicked it open. And almost reeled. 'That's... It's due in two weeks! Pete...'

'You're not supposed to know,' Pete bleated, but he'd lost control and he knew it.

'Make an appointment for me to see her today—you can spin some story to get me in there.'

'Max—'

'Now!'

'But it's all confidential.' Protest getting weaker.

'Until your clinic screwed up!'

'I'll get to the bottom of it,' Pete promised, but Max had picked up the phone and handed it to him.

'Getting to the bottom of it might protect your clinic in the future, but it's not doing a damn thing for me or this woman. Phone her!'

Pete stared at him for a long, helpless moment—and then made the call.

'Jess will give you the details,' he said as he set down the receiver and slumped back down in his chair. 'And leave Jess your information so I can keep in touch with you. That's if I can't find an unsealed window and take a leap from it.'

'You're on the second floor—you'd probably only break a leg.'

Slipping her feet back into the sandals she'd discarded under her desk, Joey heaved herself upright so she could walk out through the waiting room with her favourite patient. With her arm around the just-teenager's shoulders, she opened the door into the waiting room.

'Now, you behave yourself,' she said to Jacqui. 'Go to your own GP if your insulin levels are playing up and phone me if you're worried about anything at all. You've got both my numbers.'

'Thanks, Joey,' Jacqui responded, turning to kiss the specialist on the cheek. 'You take care yourself and have a rest before the baby arrives.' She grinned, then added, 'That's if there *is* only one!'

Smiling at the girl's remarks, Joey saw her out and was about to return to her office to check who was next on her patient list when she registered the man sitting in the corner of the waiting room.

A tense man, although, for all his tension, there was something about him.

Something disturbing.

Physically disturbing.

Special...

She continued into her office, hoping she hadn't been caught in mid-step, gazing at him instead of ignoring his presence.

But she obviously *hadn't* ignored his presence for it seemed as if every detail of his physical appearance had registered in her brain.

Even sitting, she'd been able to tell he was tall—a rangy man, with brownish-reddish hair. A swatch of it hung across a high forehead. Dark eyebrows above eyes that had seemed to be studying her, a fine, neat nose and lips—

Surely to God she hadn't just noticed his lips—hadn't noticed how well shaped they were...

Pregnancy brain!

She'd put it down to that—as she put all the silly things she was doing lately down to it.

Settling carefully behind her desk, she lifted her phone.

'There's a man in the waiting room,' she muttered to Meryl, her receptionist and the mainstay in her life right now.

'He's from the fertility clinic—some kind of rep, I suppose. They phoned and made an appointment for the end of the day.'

'End of the day? He's going to sit there while I see another four patients?'

'Apparently,' Meryl said, sounding so completely unfazed by the man's presence that Joey realised she'd have to pull herself together.

Difficult when every time she brought a patient in, or walked a family to the door, she'd see the man.

So?

She was beautiful!

He wasn't sure why this should surprise him, but it did. Dark hair and pale, creamy skin—hugely pregnant and looking very tired, but still beautiful.

The receptionist had told him he couldn't get an appointment until the end of the day and suggested he go off and get himself a coffee somewhere, but he'd felt he needed to stay—to see her—to hear the chat in the waiting room. It had all been positive. In fact, from all accounts she was an angel set down on earth, a miracle worker, and so kind, so caring, so...

He'd certainly got the picture her patients and their parents painted of her—seen her kindness as she'd shown the young teenager out, although offering her private phone number when she was about to have a baby?

Surely that was above and beyond the call of duty!

Pete had told him she was a paediatrician, so he wasn't surprised to see the waiting room with its big cane basket full of brightly coloured toys and the prints from *Alice in Wonderland* on the walls. A welcoming, non-scary place for kids.

But it was the woman herself who drew his attention, appearing at the door to her rooms to summon in the next small patient, always greeting the child first, then the parent, ushering them in, speaking directly to the child or adolescent all the time.

Her dark hair was pulled ruthlessly back into a knot on the back of her head, but from the tendrils escaping to frame her face, or dangle enticingly down the back of her neck, he could tell it was curly.

He felt a pang of sympathy for her as she followed a little group through the door, for she'd put one hand behind her and was rubbing just above her left hip.

Thirty-eight weeks... Why was she still working?

Money worries?

A string of questions rattled in his head.

Surely he wouldn't be expected to help out financially—it was all a mistake, and *not* his mistake.

But this was his child. If she needed financial help, how could he deny it?

His child?

What *was* he thinking?

But when she appeared again, he found himself staring, riveted by the bulging belly.

That was *his* baby in there.

The baby he'd decided he wasn't ever going to have for a whole fleet of excellent reasons.

This woman was having *his* baby.

His gut churned, then she glanced his way, flashed a smile at him and other bits of him reacted as well.

From a smile?

He smiled back although it was probably such a poor effort she might not have recognised it. But here he was, the man who, not so many hours ago, had made the final, definite 'no children in my future' decision, getting twinges of attraction—well, more than twinges—towards a woman carrying his child.

She'd been doing okay until he'd smiled. Admittedly, she'd sneaked a glance at him every time she'd walked into the waiting room, but apart from registering that he was a very attractive man—and her body registering the same thing in a most inappropriate manner for someone eight-and-a half-months pregnant—she really hadn't been taking *that* much notice.

The smile changed everything.

The smile made her think of things she'd long given up considering.

Like sex?

It had to be her hormones, all out of sync now she was getting so close to giving birth. The man was a total stranger—someone she'd never see again in her life. And so what if he was talking to Sam Wainwright, a hyperactive six-year-old, and actually calming him down...

But the smile had lightened the tension she'd read earlier on his face, and revealed strong white teeth, framed by those well-shaped lips—

Get out of here! Get your mind back on the job. Do not go out the door again—get Meryl to send the next patient in.

Disobeying the orders from the sensible part of her brain, Joey pushed herself to her feet and went to the door.

'Your turn, Sam,' she said, pretending to a professionalism she was far from feeling, her eyes drawn to the man who now was pulling coins from behind Sam's ear.

'Can Max come in with me and Mum?' Sam asked, smiling up at the man, who, fortunately for Joey as she'd been struck dumb, smiled at the boy and explained it wasn't his turn yet.

Of course his voice would be just that tad husky, *just* the kind of male voice that had always got her in.

Joey closed her eyes and prayed for sanity.

A little bit of sanity—surely not too much to ask for!

It came, in reaction to Sam seizing one of her legs and hugging hard, protesting that he didn't want her to go away, even for a little while.

Sensing he was genuinely upset—and assuming she'd fall over if she tried to walk—Joey eased Sam off her leg and squatted, uncomfortably, so she could look into his freckled face.

'But I have to go to hospital to have the baby, then stay home to look after it for a bit,' she reminded him. 'We talked about it, and you know Dr Austin, who'll be seeing you while I'm away.'

She ran her hand over his hair, and in a moment of complete insanity added, 'Maybe once I have the baby, you can come and visit me in hospital and meet it.'

She was about to struggle back to an upright position when a firm hand with long, strong fingers grasped her elbow and helped her up, the husky voice murmuring, 'And think what havoc he could wreak in a maternity ward,' in her ear, as he made sure she was balanced before releasing her arm.

But she wasn't thinking of Sam, or the chaos he could cause. She was trying very hard to work out why the touch of a stranger had made the hair on the back of her neck stand up and a shiver travel down her spine.

The kind of shiver she hadn't felt for seven years...

The kind of shiver David's touch had given her...

Somehow she managed to get Sam and his long-suffering mother through the door and close it behind them, but the feel of the man's fingers on her arm lingered, and something very like excitement skittered along her nerves.

He should leave right now, Max told himself. He'd seen the woman. Pete could contact her about the mistake. Even from the small interactions with her patients that he'd witnessed, he could tell she was competent and caring.

That was really all he needed to know. The baby was nothing to do with him.

So why were his eyes drawn to her belly whenever she entered the room?

Why did he feel the gut-wrench thing—the 'that's my baby in there' reaction—whenever he looked at her?

Because she was attractive?

Because he was drawn to her in some in explicable way?

Because he was having an almost primeval reaction to the news that this was *his baby*?

All those reasons were dumb. He could go now, forget this had ever happened, and if Pete told her—*when* Pete told her—about the mix-up, he needn't mention who the father was.

As for the woman—well, she *was* attractive, there was no denying that, but she wouldn't want him interfering. A woman with a child deserved stability and certainty in her life. She was a widow. She was beautiful, desirable, ripe to meet someone who could make her happy again. And if he was on the scene…

He was way ahead of himself. Thinking, stupidly, of relationships? He didn't need to go there. A man who'd already let down two women he'd loved, and who'd loved him, couldn't be trusted not to hurt a third. And to hurt a woman with a child was unthinkable.

CHAPTER TWO

THE WAITING ROOM was suddenly empty.

He still had time to leave, but when the door opened, and the tired, very pregnant but still beautiful woman walked out, he couldn't move, couldn't do anything but stare at her.

'Joanne McMillan,' she said, holding out her hand,

Suddenly aware of his own manners—bad ones that he'd stayed sitting—he surged to his feet and stepped towards her, tripping on a toy he hadn't noticed on the floor, and all but crash-tackling the woman to the floor.

Great start!

She was far more with it than him—stepping to one side but putting out a hand to steady him as he regained his balance.

'Sorry! Max Winthrop,' he muttered, grasping her free hand—the other still holding his arm.

And for the second time in the morning he was dumbstruck.

Her eyes were blue—not pale and wishy-washy blue but a clear, almost violet blue.

Mesmerising.

'You made an appointment?'

She'd dropped her hand from his arm, and it was probably just politeness that she hadn't let go of the one he was clasping.

He had the weirdest sensation that something was passing between them, bearing a warmth he didn't understand.

Of course, there was a good chance he'd completely lost his marbles. Shock could do that.

'Meryl tells me you're from the clinic. Is it just a polite visit to check if I'm okay?'

He looked into the blue eyes, drowned in the blueness, stepped back a little but somehow kept hold of her hand.

He couldn't tell her, couldn't destroy this woman's happiness because that's what still shone through the tiredness—happiness and a little excitement.

Was she really standing in her waiting room, holding the hand of a complete stranger?

Studying the complete stranger as if it was important to take in every detail of his features?

Now he was closer and she could see the fine lines fanning out from his eyes, the smile grooves bracketing his lips.

She probably should keep her eyes off the lips, and reclaim her hand...

She managed both, though how she wasn't sure for the man seemed to have cast some kind of spell over her, so they'd stood in a time-proof bubble for who knew how long.

'You're from the clinic? Is this just a courtesy call?'

Somehow she'd managed the repeat the question she'd asked earlier, pretending to a normality she was far from feeling. But she'd no sooner spoken than the man turned pale, pain of some kind straining the features she'd found so mesmeric.

'Yes! No!'

He'd stepped back a little, which was just as well because his close proximity had certainly added to the strange mix of sensations she'd been experiencing.

Although his confusion was now transmitting itself to her in definite twinges of anxiety.

'Yes, or no, which is it?' she asked, producing a smile to cover the anxiety.

'Oh, hell, I've no idea. I should walk right out the door, right now—out the door and out of your life.'

Out of my life? 'But you're not actually *in* my life,' Joey pointed out. 'In my rooms, yes, but hardly in my life!'

Max Winthrop—she was almost certain that was the name he'd given—groaned, turning even paler.

'Perhaps you should sit down,' Joey told him, and placing her hand very carefully on his arm she guided him back to where he'd been sitting earlier.

Touching him was probably a mistake as all the sensations she'd experienced earlier returned a thousandfold.

This was insanity. The man was a stranger. Okay, so he was an attractive stranger, but in truth she'd met many better-looking men, knew a dozen of them and had dated quite a few.

With absolutely no physical reaction whatsoever...

Not since David!

She patted her stomach and tried to think.

The clinic!

And for the first time since Meryl had mentioned the clinic, the man and the attraction were forgotten, and she felt a surge of panic.

'There's nothing wrong, is there?'

She'd been looking down at him, but now he stood up and put his hand on her arm again.

'Perhaps we should both sit down,' he said, so softly, so gently, the surge turned into a roaring tsunami of fear, invading every cell of her body.

Both hands now protectively cradling her belly, she stared at the man.

'Tell me,' she demanded.

Had she lost colour that he almost forced her into the chair? Sat her down then settled beside her, his hand still grasping her arm?

It was comforting, that hand, but why should she need comforting?

'Talk!' she ordered, trying to read his face—a strong face, unused, she was sure, to uncertainty or confusion, although both emotions seemed to be in evidence right now.

He opened his mouth as if to respond then closed it again, but not before it had attracted her attention to the extent that she had to confirm it was a very nice mouth—and little lines she'd noticed earlier were evidence that he smiled a lot.

But he was not smiling now.

Was he so uncomfortable sitting beside her that he needed to move to squat, awkwardly, in front of her, the way she did when speaking to a small patient?

Or did he need to see her face while he said whatever he had to say?

Fear was creeping into the panic now and her heart was thudding in her chest.

'Please,' she whispered.

He took her hands, both hands—and even in her panicky state she felt a shiver of reaction. He turned them in his, before looking into her eyes.

'Look,' he finally said, 'I haven't the faintest clue how to tell you this, but the clinic said they would contact you, and as far as I could see, that would be a disaster. Maybe it's a disaster anyway but at least now you'll see exactly what's happened. You deserve to know and I need to tell you.'

He wasn't making any sense but he did seem genuinely concerned, which, together with the talk of the clinic, had the nerves in Joey's tummy heading straight for riot mode.

'Perhaps you could just blurt it out,' she suggested as the tension in the air between them reached seismic proportions.

Just blurt it out, that's rich! Max muttered to himself. Here's this stunning woman, ready to pop any minute, and a total stranger walks in...

Aware the silence had already taken too long, he took an extra minute to study Joanne—Joey, her small patients had called her—McMillan.

And was drawn again to her eyes, wide apart so she seemed, even in her bewildered state, to be constantly surprised.

But it was the pale, creamy skin that made her lovely to look at—he hoped the baby got that...

What was he thinking? As if it mattered what kind of skin the baby had? It wasn't as if it really was his baby!

Was it?

'The thing is...' he said, as thoughts of the baby reminded him of his mission. *And* of the mess they were in.

'The thing is...'

He stopped, stood up before his knees gave out and slumped back into the chair beside her. Sitting beside her was bad enough as far as the attraction thing was concerned, but looking up into those eyes—no wonder he couldn't think!

'The thing is...' she prompted, reasonably gently considering his eruption into her life and the tension she must be feeling.

To make matters worse, she then turned towards him and reached out to rest one hand on his.

'The thing is, you're having my baby. There, it's said. Now all we have to do is work out where we go from here.'

She didn't reply—hardly surprising!—but the slim fingers that he'd wrapped in his hand seemed to lose all warmth and he turned anxiously towards her.

'You're okay? You're not going to faint or anything?'

'Of course I'm not okay,' she snapped. 'What are you? Some kind of a madman who goes around scaring pregnant woman? Does it give you a kick to see someone in shock?'

She leaned forward as best she could, given her shape, but she didn't retrieve her hand. In fact, her fingers were now clinging to his, as if to a lifeline. Fortunately the re-

ceptionist reappeared at that moment, and Max turned to
her for help.

'She's had a shock—a hot drink, tea if she drinks it,
and lots of sugar.'

'No sugar!'

The change to the order reassured Max that Joey Mc-
Millan was recovering fast.

Which was good in one way, but it meant explanations
were in order.

Not only explanations but also some kind of discussion
over the future, although what that future could be was
hard to envision.

Impossible really.

Although…

The thought was so unexpected he stopped breathing for
a moment, and turned it this way and that in his head before
giving it consideration. It remained the same—a conviction
that, having had his own father walk out when he was five,
he *should* have some involvement in his child's upbringing.

Shouldn't he?

It was nuts but his thoughts were racing at a million
miles an hour.

His mother would be a grandmother.

The thought held him riveted. He shuddered as he considered what his mother and sisters would say if he *didn't*
accept the baby as his own. In fact, they'd be delighted
something had happened to curtail what they saw as his
irresponsibly nomadic, and often dangerous, lifestyle.

Sisters!

And *that* made him wonder if Joey knew the sex of the
child. A boy would be fun but, then, little girls—

Was he *really* considering being a father to this child?

Well, shouldn't he be?

He stifled a groan. He'd been so intent on getting to this
woman and telling her the unfortunate truth in person that
he hadn't given a thought to the implications for himself.

His stomach clenched, but it was the confusion in his mind that really worried him. Confusion over the baby but, worse, confusion over his reactions to this woman…

Joey waited until Meryl brought the tea. Meryl headed back behind her desk and turned her attention to her computer. Her presence made things feel…almost normal. She straightened up, retrieved the hand she'd carelessly left lying in the man's warm paw, took several sips of hot liquid and turned to face the stranger.

Max something, he had said?

'If you're not mad, then presumably you have some explanation for your bizarre statement,' she said, hoping she sounded stronger than she felt, which, right now, was extremely shaky.

And totally confused.

And upset? *Yes,* she thought, unbelievably upset, so upset she didn't dare go there. That this wasn't David's baby…

And still, crazy as it might be, she was drawn to this man in some inexplicable fashion.

'I do have an explanation,' he said. 'But it's long and involved and you've obviously just finished a full day at work and probably need a rest and food, so we don't have to do this now.'

She stared at him in disbelief.

'You think I could rest?' she demanded, and hoped the words hadn't come out too shrill. She hated sounding shrill.

'Well, food and somewhere comfortable to sit,' he suggested, and Joey realised he was right.

'I was intending to go straight home, it's not far,' she said, immediately regretting it as she realised she was inviting a total stranger into her house.

'You can't go inviting total strangers into your house,' the man scolded, right on cue.

Joey sighed. She was tired and her back ached and her

feet hurt and all she wanted to do was go home and sit in a nice warm bath.

Maybe snooze in it until the water got cold... Forget about dramas like a stranger claiming to be the father to her child.

But she couldn't forget. She pulled herself together—or as together as she was likely to get at the moment.

'Just give Meryl all your details and show her some identification so she can tell the police about who murdered me if I don't get in touch with her in the morning.'

The man looked surprised, then worried, then unhappy, but in the end Meryl saved the day.

'I've already done an internet search on him,' she piped up. 'I know, it's not my business but I'm nosey and he's cute.' She grinned. 'He has nothing to do with the IVF clinic.' She frowned at Max. 'That's false pretences when you made the appointment. But he's still a doctor, but mainly he works for overseas aid organisations. He's in the front line of infectious disease research in underdeveloped countries. The organisation he works for has his picture on their website so I know it's him. Take a look if you like.' She swung the monitor to face Joey. 'Apparently he teaches as well as works hands on. There's a profile of him on the page; he climbs mountains in between plagues. He looks like an adrenaline junkie. Maybe a bit mad but harmless.'

'A bit mad?' Joey echoed, staring at her receptionist in shock. 'Did you hear any of his conversation? Do you know what he came to tell me?'

Meryl looked embarrassed.

'Well, he did kind of explain a little of it when he came in. He asked me to stay in case you needed someone with you. I know it's a shock, Joey, but I think he's okay.'

Joey glared at her receptionist.

'Well, thanks a lot. I'm going home now, so you can go too.'

She knew she shouldn't be snapping at Meryl, but it was as if the pair had formed a conspiracy of some kind. The worst of it was, she knew, very, very deep down inside, that the bombshell he'd just dropped on her *could* be possible. Accidents could happen in any medical process or procedure—

But not this time! No way!

Maybe back in the beginning of IVF and sperm freezing, but not these days. Surely not.

'Well, come on,' she grumped at the bearer of bad tidings, 'let's go to my place so you can explain yourself.'

Politeness dictated he help her up but as Max stood and held out his hand, he felt as if he was poking it into the cave of a very hungry grizzly bear. This particular pregnant woman was certainly angry enough to bite.

He eased her to her feet, grasping her elbow to steady her once she was upright, feeling her softness, seeing the deep cleft between her engorged breasts, feeling a stirring that was way beyond inappropriate.

Half of him was unable to stop considering her belly, feeling quite possessive about a child he'd been determined not to have, while the other half of him yelled that this was madness—getting involved was madness. Hadn't he already figured out that long-term relationships weren't for him? And what was a child if it wasn't very, very, very long-term?

He pushed his brain past the warring voices in his head, seeking a little scrap of sanity.

'Do you drive to your place?' he asked, worried about her wellbeing after the shock, and wishing he had a car himself so he could take her wherever she wanted to go.

Madness! The angry voice in his head declared.

She turned her head and smiled—well, almost smiled.

'No, I walk. It's my daily exercise, walking to and from work, climbing the stairs rather than taking the elevator.'

'This suite's on the fourteenth floor.'

The protest was automatic and this time she did smile, stirring things inside him once again.

'Not here, but at home. You'll see.'

And he did. Following her up flight after flight of stairs in an old building near the top of the city terrace that provided consulting suites for most of the city's specialists.

'I didn't know these old buildings still had flats in them,' he said when she stopped at the top of the final flight and pulled out an old-fashioned-looking brass key to unlock a heavy wooden door.

'Not many of them do,' she replied, and he realised, as no hint of breathlessness sounded in the words, that she must be supremely fit for someone almost at term.

Inside he looked around with wonder at the high ceilings, the spacious living/dining room, the wide hall with doors that must open into bedrooms off to one side.

And the view!

Drawn to the wide windows, he gazed down at the city spread out beneath, the muddy green-brown river meandering through it, and out to the suburbs, tree-lined streets and red roofs.

'It's amazing,' he said, and this time the smile lit up her face.

'It's my family home,' she admitted rather shyly. 'Everyone tells me I'm mad to consider living here with a baby, what with the stairs and all, but my mother managed and my father's mother before her so I don't see why I can't. Especially these days when I can do all my grocery shopping online and there's an ancient dumb waiter the delivery man can use with his loads of foodstuffs.'

She'd walked into the living room and sunk down onto a comfortable-looking lounge, kicking off her sandals and lifting her legs to rest them along the seat.

'Sit,' she said, but the word was more a plea than a command. She sounded exhausted and he cursed himself for hitting her with this shock after she'd had a long day at work.

But better him than the clinic, surely?

He stayed standing, studying her, not knowing where to go next in this impossible conversation—not wanting to hurt this woman any more than he already had but knowing the conversation had to continue.

'Can I get you something? Go out and get us a meal? Or get *you* a meal? You're probably far too tired to be worrying about this other business right now.'

She looked better smiling than frowning, he decided as she said, 'I thought we'd established that there's no way I can rest or relax until we've sorted out what you so glibly call this "other business"! You're talking about wrecking my entire life here, do you realise that?'

It was Max's turn to sink down into a chair, where he sighed, then held his head in his hands for a few minutes, then sighed again before looking up at her.

'I know, and I did consider not telling you at all. I know people have this obsession about truth, but a lot of truth just hurts.'

His face was shadowed but Joey read sorrow in it and wondered just how badly he'd been hurt by some truth in the past. And for some reason beyond her understanding, it hurt her that he'd been hurt.

She really *was* a mess!

'I suppose, both morally and ethically, you need to know,' he acknowledged. 'But I thought I should come in person—explain in person.'

She couldn't help the frown that must be causing permanent creases in her forehead.

'I don't understand any of this, but I'm assuming you somehow found out, or think you found out, that I was inseminated with your sperm instead of David's. But the checks and balances at the IVF centre are so complex, it can't happen.'

'Exactly what I thought,' Max told her gloomily, 'and in case inside that calm exterior you're raging about yelling and threatening to sue, I've already done enough of that for both of us. Problem is I can't help feeling doctors get a bad enough press without patients suing them so I wouldn't really like to go that far.'

He'd kind of run out of words, so he looked hopefully at Joey.

Nothing!

He ploughed on.

'Can you tell me why you used frozen sperm? I know the name on the files when they were finally tracked down was McMillan. That was or is your husband?'

For a moment he didn't think she'd answer. Her eyes were unfocussed and he guessed she was looking inwards—to a not very happy place if he read her expression correctly.

'David had a headache. A bad headache.' She spoke slowly, quietly, offering the words one by one as if each one still caused pain. 'He was diagnosed with an aggressive, inoperable brain tumour and given six weeks to live. We'd been married a month. I didn't want him to do the frozen sperm thing. If I couldn't have *him*, I certainly didn't want his baby. I was angry—at him for being sick, and at myself for handling it so badly. Angry at the whole world.'

She paused, looking around the room, probably remembering her beloved husband in it with her—probably regretting her anger…

'Anyway he did it, saying that, in time, he fully expected me to find someone else to love and marry. That was what he really wanted for me, he said, but if that didn't happen, then he'd like me to have the option of having his baby. I could have someone of his—some part of him—to give me the love I deserved. That was how he put it. And it's been there, in the back of my mind, ever since. Then last year I thought I can't keep the sperm forever. If I don't do it now…' She shrugged. 'Anyway, I just did. I wanted to and I did. But now…what have I done? A baby that's not David's…'

She rested her head back on the arm of the couch and closed her eyes, as if telling this tragic story had stolen her last reserves of energy, leaving her too exhausted to wipe away the tears that leaked, slow and full, from beneath her eyelids.

CHAPTER THREE

HIS FINGERS ACHED to wipe those tears away, but she was a stranger—a stranger he'd just hurt beyond any understanding, which meant touching her was out of the question.

And particularly out of the question given how previous touches—casual, helpful touches—had affected him.

Be practical. Practical was good. He could do practical!

Food—she undoubtedly needed food.

Max stood up and went in search of the kitchen, not hard to find as it was right at the end of the hall. A tall, walk-in pantry offered a packet of crackers and the refrigerator cheese, grapes and tiny tomatoes. He sliced some cheese, found a plate and set out his offerings. He took a bottle of mineral water from the refrigerator and poured a glass, added ice, and carried the plate and glass into the living room, setting it down on a small table beside the couch.

'Eat!' he ordered, and to his surprise she opened her eyes and smiled at him. It was a wan smile, but it was still a smile.

He definitely liked her smile.

'Only if we share,' she said, waving her hand towards the plate, so he took a cracker, and a chunk of cheese and a grape, but knew he wouldn't eat them, his tension over the conversation that lay ahead making his body so uptight he doubted it would accept anything in the way of food.

'So!' she said, after she'd demolished half the plate of food while he'd surreptitiously wrapped his morsels in his handkerchief and poked it in his pocket. 'Tell me what makes you think this is your baby.'

She patted her belly protectively but in a matter-of-fact way, and Max guessed if she spoke to the unborn child at all, it would be as an adult—in a normal conversation. A sensible, intelligent woman, as well as being beautiful.

But he had a tale to tell...

'I went to the lab this morning—'

'Brilliant Babies, or whatever silly name they're calling themselves now?' she queried.

'Babies First,' Max corrected. 'Yes.'

He stalled again.

'And you went because...?'

Joey asked the question and sighed inside. Was she going to have to drag every syllable of the story out of this man? She hoped not. She'd been tired before he'd dropped his unbelievable bombshell—now she was exhausted.

She ate another couple of grapes, hoping their sugar content might help.

'I wanted to have my sperm destroyed,' he said finally. 'The frozen stuff. It's been stored there now for seven years and they'd sent a bill recently or I'd have forgotten about it altogether. The quality of the frozen sperm probably deteriorates with time, but it wasn't all that. I guess it was an acceptance that I wasn't cut out to be a family man. It's probably genetic. My father thought he could be, but my sisters tell me he was never happy when he was at home. But when he finally cut and ran, well, to me it was so hurtful that I realised I'd have been better off never having had a father.'

Joey knew she was frowning again. No wonder, considering he was telling her his life story, rather than explaining what had happened at the clinic.

'But if that's how you felt,' she said, 'why freeze your sperm in the first place? It can't have been a donation because that clinic doesn't take donations and, anyway, in places where they do, they're stored separately. Did you think you were ill?'

She stopped, because it had suddenly struck her that she was having a conversation with a virtual stranger about his sperm.

Beyond weird!

'Well?' she demanded when he still didn't answer.

'I'd been diagnosed with non-Hodgkin lymphoma. And I had a fiancée at the time. I was young and optimistic enough to think I could make a go of marriage and family.'

He paused for a moment, then added, with more irony than bitterness, 'I was still optimistic, or perhaps foolish, to think the same thing the second time I became engaged.'

The second time?

She *had* to ask!

'I can perhaps understand losing one fiancée—particularly if she couldn't handle your being ill—but two? Or were there more?'

He didn't answer for a moment. Why should he when his love life really wasn't any of her business? But he didn't look stricken by pain at the loss of these women, but more thoughtful than anything else.

Until he frowned.

'No, you're wrong. My first fiancée did stick around—for quite a lot of my treatment. But I was treated very aggressively and being around someone who's sick all the time isn't much fun. Plus I was a terrible patient. We were both young. When she decided to move on, it was the right decision for both of us.'

Good for him, defending her, Joey thought, although she was well aware this conversation was nothing more than a delaying tactic.

A delay she needed right now...

'And the second?'

'She was a stunner,' he said simply. 'I was over illness,

over everything and I fell hard. But maybe I'm not cut out for marriage. She was planning the wedding, planning babies, planning life and suddenly things started to close in. So I went to climb Everest,' he said, startling Joey so much she had to straighten up from her comfy slump.

'You went off to climb Everest? So Meryl's right, you are a little mad!'

She shook her head, trying to clear the vision of a huge snow-capped mountain so she could concentrate on what really mattered in the conversation.

But mountains that big were hard to shift.

'So did you?'

'Yep. I managed to annoy my fiancée enough for her to call it off. I thought she'd understand because she knew climbing Everest had always been a dream, it was just that after—'

'Forget the fiancée! Did you climb the mountain? Did you make it to the top?'

Even the idea of such a feat sent a thrill down her spine and she looked at the attractive stranger with new eyes. Not that she hadn't been looking at him fairly closely since he'd first appeared...

Hormones—it had to be hormones...

He smiled, but the faraway look in his eyes told her he was back there again—back in those mighty mountains.

'No, but I knew all along I wouldn't be going to the top. I was support crew, and for me it was enough to be there— to be on the mountain right up to the last camp, before the final assault. It was magic.'

'And hard and tough and dangerous as well?'

He smiled.

'So's beating cancer,' he said. 'But for me, right from the diagnosis, it was a goal to work towards. I had a friend planning a climb and that gave me the motivation not only to get through the treatment but after it to do the training and build myself up to peak physical fitness—the kind that was needed if I wanted to be included in the team.'

'But the second fiancée?'

'I'd thought I could settle down, build a general practice here. It almost happened.'

Joey studied the man who'd catapulted into her life while she tried to make sense of all he was telling her. There were loose ends everywhere and she wasn't even up to the mistake part.

Although she wasn't in that much of a hurry to get to the mistake part. She'd rather go on thinking the baby inside her was David's—sweet, gentle David's—for as long as possible.

'But it didn't happen?' she asked, before she could get melancholy over David again.

Green eyes studied her in turn and she knew he was tossing up whether to tell the truth or offer a vague evasion.

'Hmm,' he finally said, 'well…'

'Spit it out,' she ordered. 'It can't be any worse than the "you're having my baby" line you used earlier.'

'It was definitely my fault,' he began, and she knew he'd decided on the truth. 'I was due to be back in Australia a month before the wedding but, coming down, before we'd reached base camp where we were to fly out from, we had news of an avalanche on another part of the mountain—'

'Involving other climbers?'

The man nodded.

'We were closest, I'm a doctor, it was a fair climb to reach them. The snow and ice around them were so unstable we couldn't risk a helicopter rescue so getting the survivors out was tricky. Once they were handed over to the professionals we went back.'

The look on his face told her why. There'd been fatalities and he and his fellow climbers had brought out the bodies as well.

'Some people find it's easier to accept if they can bury their loved ones.'

The quiet sentence confirmed her guess. But the wedding?

'So just how long was it before you returned to your fiancée?' Joey asked, as the meaning of this rambling excuse became clear.

'I was in touch whenever I could be,' he said defensively. 'Emails, texts, phone calls, you know how easy it is these days.'

'So what happened?' she asked, deciding to get back on track, although she'd really have liked to ask more about the mountain—both climbing and mountain-rescue work.

Rescue work.

Meryl had mentioned that. It sounded...intriguing.

'I was dumped by text,' Max replied. 'It was waiting when we brought the survivors down, only weeks after leaving the base of Everest, about the time I should have been home. She'd met someone who loved her more than mountains, someone who wasn't the most selfish person ever put on earth.'

'She put all that in a text?'

Her visitor grinned.

'Not quite. That's just what I took "Gt stfd am kpg ring" to mean. She'd told me the most selfish man on earth part many times and I've since heard her version of the story. Anyway, I went on another rescue mission to heal my broken heart—or maybe in the hope of breaking my neck because of my broken heart—and I've been...wandering since. Involving myself more and more with the problems of remote communities. Seeing how infectious diseases can decimate them. Trying to do something about it.'

'And your lymphoma?'

His smile lit up the room.

'All clear!'

Yes, non-Hodgkin lymphoma was like that—not like aggressive brain tumours, Joey thought sadly, remembering back. Remembering David insisting on freezing sperm in case she ever wanted it—telling her the best option would be her finding someone else to love, to make a family with. He'd been so sure she would…

Max watched the shadows chase across her face and knew she'd been thinking about her husband, who hadn't left her for his own selfish reasons but had been snatched from her by death.

Why hadn't she found someone else? he wondered. She was a lovely-looking woman, obviously intelligent and interested in things outside her own world—hadn't she shown interest in the mountains?

But 'Yes,' was all he said, and let the silence settle between them.

She picked up a cracker and used it to push a piece of cheese around the plate, then poked at a grape, before looking up at him.

'We're down to the nitty-gritty now, aren't we?' There was so much sadness in her voice; he wanted to go and sit beside her, to put his arms around her and hold her tight—to assure her everything would be all right, although he knew full well nothing would ever be the same for her again.

Or him, if the strange stuff going on inside him was any indication…

He sighed. Holding her wasn't an option, so he'd best get on with it.

'Do you remember anything of the day your husband went to the clinic?'

She looked at him, a little frown forming between her eyebrows.

'Not really. I would have been angry—I was always angry back then—although…'

He waited, seeing the frown deepen as she dug back in her memory to a time she'd rather forget.

'Something happened. I do remember. It was at the clinic. Some kind of fuss?'

He waited and she shook her head.

'I can't remember details—I've blanked out as much as I can of that part of my life. But there was a fuss of some kind. I remember thinking—furiously—that I might have lost him five weeks earlier than I needed to have and all because of the stupid sperm.'

She gave her belly another pat as if to excuse her words, while Max recalled the events of the morning only too clearly.

'There *was* a fuss,' he told her, although the word 'fuss' hardly covered the magnitude of it. 'A man came in with a gun. Apparently he and his wife had frozen four embryos some time earlier—there was some hereditary disease in one or other of their families and these had been tested and found free of whatever gene could cause the problem.'

'And his wife had left him?' Joey put in. 'Of course! I remember David telling me the story.'

'Exactly! Left him for another man, so the deserted husband wanted the embryos destroyed but apparently she was listed as the owner so the clinic couldn't destroy them without her say-so. He pulled out a gun, grabbed one of the laboratory staff and demanded action.'

'Just as you and David had done your thing in your discreetly curtained cubicles and come out clutching your little jars?'

She half smiled and all the attraction stuff started up in his body again. This was beyond bizarre. He had to concentrate on the story, then help this woman—who was the real victim of the clinic's mistake—in any way he could.

'Not quite, because we'd heard all the commotion and actually gone further into the lab to try to work out what we could do to help. We were in the janitor's room, with the door open so we could hear what was going on.'

He paused, then added, 'So, I met your David and,

knowing now why he was there, I can understand why he thought the best option was to rush the man. I pointed out that he might shoot his hostage before he shot David, and in the end we decided on shock tactics. Not very brave or heroic, we just filled a bucket with hot water and threw it at him, hoping for the best. In retrospect it was probably a stupid thing to do but it worked. The man was so surprised he dropped the gun to wipe the water from his face, the lab assistant he was holding fell to the floor and a lot of people pounced.'

A proper smile this time.

'I *do* remember now,' she said. 'I even remember David telling me about hiding in the cupboard with some bloke who wanted to live through his treatment so he could climb mountains.'

'We were *not* hiding. We were *planning*,' Max informed her, but he was glad to see that she was still smiling.

'So?' she asked, and he knew he'd got to the hard part.

He shifted in the very comfortable chair then faced the woman sitting opposite him, looking directly at her.

'I'm only assuming this is what happened. The clinic is still trying to work it out. But when I went there today, someone in the cryo room brought out the straws frozen in my name, but when they checked—and they do check and cross-check—the numbers on the straws were your David's. I can only assume that with all the fuss the day we were in there, someone had switched the jars—a-million-to-one chance of a mistake happening, but there it was.'

Joey could only stare at the stranger. The stranger whose baby she was, apparently, carrying.

Slowly and carefully, she went through it all in her mind and she understood that it *could* have happened.

But had it?

Shouldn't she check?

Too late now to phone the clinic—

'Shouldn't they have got in touch with me as soon

as they found out?' she demanded, as the enormity of it flooded her body. 'Didn't I deserve to be told? To have some kind of apology, some support?'

Max stood up and came across to where she sat, sitting down beside her and tentatively resting a hand on her shoulder, wanting to comfort her and not knowing how.

Wanting to hold her and tell her everything would be all right—make promises he had no right to make and that she would probably reject anyway.

He'd insisted on being the person who told her—and all because he'd wanted to check out whether she'd make a good mother. Guilt was niggling in his gut.

That had been a really big mistake. But how was he to know he'd be instantly attracted to her? Love at first sight was nonsense. He *knew* that!

'That's my fault,' he admitted, shoving the L word to the very darkest corner of his brain. 'It *was* only this afternoon, and it seemed to me you deserved to be told in person. I offered to do it. In fact...' he gave a rueful smile '...I insisted. The guy who runs the clinic went through med school with me. I didn't give him much choice. Unethical, but there it is. Once I came down from the ceiling, I figured if you had to have some of the truth, you might as well have the lot. Including who your father's baby really is.'

It was a reasonable explanation, he decided. She knew it all now. He could walk away.

But something was happening he didn't understand. On top of the attraction thing, there was bit of him that had suddenly become illogically, irrationally possessive of the baby. Possessive and responsible...

Remember, he told himself, he'd decided no kids.

'You offered to do it?' Joey prompted, and he battled to get his thoughts in order so he could get back to the conversation.

'I told them I was sure you'd be in touch with them, but I believed—I mean, the shock alone—I thought—'

'I'd have fainted, or gone into labour or—Heaven only knows how I might have reacted—am reacting…'

Joey threw up her arms and leaned back into the soft cushions at the back of the lounge, edging just a little away from the man who was causing a great deal of uncertainty in her body as well as total confusion in her mind.

'I've no idea what to think,' she said, then she turned to Max. 'Do you?'

He shrugged his broad shoulders by way of reply and she told herself it was the shock that made him seem so attractive. She'd had a shock and he was here to support her—of course he'd seem attractive.

'Not really,' he said, 'although we obviously have to think about the baby. I mean, if you don't want a baby that's not David's, his sperm is still there and you could try again. I could probably take the baby—my mother and sisters could possibly—'

'*Take the baby?*' Joey's reaction was as instinctive as a bear protecting her cub. She was staring at him in horror. 'You'd take the baby and I could just try again? This is *my* baby we're talking about. Okay, so David—or presumably you, but I'm not accepting that until I've talked to the clinic—*might* have made a contribution, but this is *my* baby!'

'The contribution is half and half,' said her visitor, who'd shifted a little away from her in obvious discomfort.

'And who's been carrying it around for months, and not having a glass of wine, and eating good food, and walking up a million steps so it stays healthy? Not to mention morning sickness and indigestion and not being able to get comfortable enough to have a decent night's sleep? Tell me that, then tell me it's half and half.'

'Well, not quite,' Max admitted, 'but it's still my baby.'

So he was one of those stubborn men, Joey thought. And then thought, irrationally, I hope our baby hasn't inherited that trait—although the green eyes would be nice…

Our baby. It was a weird thought.

'Which leaves us where?' she demanded, upset all over again now she had to worry about the baby being stubborn—and her reactions to this man.

She was mulling this over when Max replied.

'I'm not trying to take it away from you.'

'Gee, thanks.'

'But I do want to help.'

'I don't need...'

And then he had another of those light-bulb moments. Crazy, irrational, but the thought was there. A solution that would let him wander but would still give him a say.

He'd nearly done it twice. Maybe he could...

'Joey, I'm not much of a catch because I'm not around much,' he said slowly. 'I'm called away at inconvenient times. I live independently. But if we both were to be parents... If there's no one else for you... I suppose... Maybe we could get married. You know, a marriage of convenience—so the baby had a father... I could contribute—'

But Joey was staring at him as if he was out of his mind. 'Is that all marriage means to you?' she managed. She rose, her face blank with incomprehension. 'Marriage... This is nuts. No, it's beyond nuts. You come here and tell me you're my baby's father, and then you calmly decide we can say a few vows but not really mean them, and you can head off, duty done, only you'll have a child and a little wife back home? You've said you've broken off with two fiancées, and I can see their point. If marriage means so little...' She gasped and put her hand to her back. 'No. That's none of my business. You are none of my business. I don't know you and I don't want to know you. Anything my baby and I do is up to us; we don't want some phantom mountain-climbing husband and father wafting in and out of our lives when he feels like it.'

'I didn't mean—'

'No. You didn't mean because you didn't think. This has

been as almost as much a shock to you as it is to me, but the answer, believe it or not, is not to take lifetime vows. Max, you need to go.'

'I can't—'

'You don't have a choice,' she said, and gripped her back tighter. Something was… Something…

He moved forward in instinctive concern as she gasped and then buckled.

'Joey!'

'Shut up,' she managed. 'Just shut up and leave.'

But he couldn't leave. He watched in mounting concern as she collapsed back against the couch, as a strong, un-mistakeable contraction gripped her body.

Two strong contractions—one right after the other…

CHAPTER FOUR

'No!' SHE SHRIEKED. All that had gone before disappeared in a haze of shock and pain. 'This can't happen now. I'm not nearly ready and Kirstie's away, I haven't any nappies, I haven't read the book—I just *cannot* have this baby now.'

She tried to stand up mid-rant but that made matters worse, although Max Winthrop seemed to be taking it all very calmly, gripping her by the arm to make sure she didn't fall.

And as she crumbled he seemed to find strength. She was turning into a whimpering expectant mum. He was turning into a doctor.

'It's okay,' he said, infuriatingly soothingly. 'I guess it's the shock, but at thirty-eight weeks... Let's not panic.'

'I want to panic.' She was almost yelling.

'You could go and have a warm shower,' he suggested as the pain in her body eased. 'See if it settles. It could give you time out, make you feel better.'

'I might not *want* to feel better!' she muttered, but he was right. She was reasonably sure warm water *would* make her body relax, now that the scary contractions had passed.

She sat for a bit, waiting for the pain to return. Max sat by calmly. He was going nowhere. He was her own personal nightmare, she thought, but she had to concede his calmness did help.

Dumb marriage proposal or not, maybe she wasn't going to kick him out.

No more contractions. Swearing to herself, she headed for the bathroom where she took one look at the big, old-fashioned claw-footed bath and knew a bath would be a thousand times better than a shower.

'I'll have a bath,' she muttered to herself, but he had obviously followed her—to make sure she was okay—and had heard the mutter.

'Just be careful you don't slip. Yell if you need help getting out.'

'Fine.' She shut the door fast. The idea of this man—this stranger—helping her out of the bath in all her naked glory was causing weird sensations in the pit of her stomach.

Although maybe that was something to do with the contractions...

She ran water into the tub, stripped off her clothes and dumped them in the clothes basket.

Aaah! It was pure bliss to slide beneath the warm water, to rest her head back on the edge of the bath, to close her eyes and relax.

Well, almost relax.

Total relaxation, with all the mess in her head, was impossible.

And what had that man said?

Perhaps they should get married?

A marriage of convenience?

Convenient for whom?

He can't have meant it! It was the shock talking. For he must be as shocked by the news as she was.

Total strangers didn't get married, conveniently or otherwise, even if they shared a child.

Did they?

And if he wasn't around much, what was the point? A husband off climbing or off rescuing...

But he *was* attractive.

What *was* she thinking? What she'd said to him was true. It was totally nuts.

So why was she thinking of it? Loneliness? Fear of what lay before her?

She should forget his nonsense and think about what lies immediately ahead. Should she be feeling more contractions? How soon? She *had* flicked through a little gem of a book, *The Don't Panic Guide to Birth* by a very experienced midwife, Fiona McArthur, who'd not only delivered countless babies but had five herself.

Fiona would know, she decided, and she'd have time to read it properly when she got out of the bath and before the contractions got too bad.

'You okay in there?'

The male voice reminded her she wasn't alone and for some reason she found that very comforting.

'I'm fine,' she said. 'I'll be out in a minute. Please help yourself to anything you can find in the kitchen to eat.'

'I'm already doing that,' he replied. 'I'll have a cup of tea and some sandwiches ready for you when you get out.'

Again she had a niggly feeling deep inside, and she was pretty sure it wasn't pain.

You're not used to having a man in the house, she told herself, when further analysis of the niggle suggested it had been his voice that had caused it. Just as his hand on her arm, earlier, had made her blood go warm.

Appalled by her thoughts, she clambered out, grateful that her walking and stair-climbing had kept her fit enough to be able to do it unaided.

But what to put on? While she was thinking, another contraction hit. Fifteen minutes. Okay, she'd have to go to the hospital soon. What to wear to the hospital was just one of a long list of things she'd been going to ask Kirstie, who had promised to be her birth partner but who was currently hundreds of miles away in Sydney.

Panic threatened, but she pushed it away, although not

far enough. Her heart was fluttering wildly in her chest. Pain. Fear. Hormones?

Think!

The fleecy tracksuit—wasn't that what she'd decided to wear? Though she'd get hot—labouring women got very hot and sweaty—but that was—

'Are you sure you're okay?'

He must be right outside the door. Joey wrapped herself in a towel and opened it.

'I don't know what to wear,' she all but wailed, and was disgusted with herself when she heard the pathetic words. This wasn't her at all. She was *woman*, she was strong, she *did* not wail—or yelp, or shriek, for that matter.

'Come on, we'll sort it out,' he said, in such a matter-of-fact manner she let him take her by the hand and lead her into her bedroom.

Had he explored while she was in the bath?

Did it matter?

'Sit on the bed,' he said. 'Undies first, I should think. They're in one of these drawers, I imagine.'

Joey stared in astonishment at the sight of a man she didn't know delving into her underwear drawers.

At least it diverted the panic.

She really should object, tell him to get out, that she could manage perfectly well on her own. But somehow she knew she couldn't, and right now it was intensely comforting having someone tell her what to do, even if it was a man, and a stranger at that!

He held up a bra—not a delicate, lacy, sexy and romantic confection but a sturdy, very basic and utterly unattractive maternity bra.

She nodded and he tossed it to her, then opened a few other drawers, coming up with an equally unbecoming pair of knickers.

She nodded again, feeling her cheeks heat as the reality of the situation wound its way into her consciousness.

Surely this was the height of embarrassment, although the man was handling it with such detachment it couldn't be worrying him.

Sisters—he'd mentioned he had sisters—maybe that helped.

And he was a doctor, after all.

'I'll leave you to get dressed,' he said, 'or would you like help?

Help putting her massive boobs into a maternity bra? No, thank you very much!

'I'll manage,' she said, clutching her underwear and the towel and wishing that he would go as her embarrassment had reached almost crippling levels.

'I'll be right outside,' he assured her and smiled. 'You know, I'd decided children weren't for me, but now this has happened, it's as if something's snapped inside me. Here I am thinking how lucky this is. To think I'll be around when my baby's born!'

Forget embarrassment and panic, now she wanted to throw something at the man, but he'd disappeared, pulling the door to but leaving it a little ajar, presumably in case she needed him.

A caring man?

Not too caring to go off climbing mountains for years while his fiancée waited at home.

And hadn't this mess started when he'd gone to the clinic to have his sperm destroyed because he didn't want children?

So why was he getting excited about *his* baby being born?

The man was a contradiction but the option of him not being there when the baby was born was not very appealing. Well, not him exactly but not having *someone* there beside her.

As an only child of parents who'd died not long after David, she no longer had family. Kirstie was away, her other close friend, Lissa, had three kids and her husband was overseas, David's parents were overseas—and she doubted the couple, now in their seventies, would want to watch a baby being born, even if they didn't know it wasn't their grandchild. Oh, dear heaven, what was she going to tell them?

She dropped the towel and struggled into her bra and knickers, found a big T-shirt she slept in in summer so she could take off the tracksuit and still be relatively decent when push, almost literally, came to shove, then picked out her warm red tracksuit and pulled it on. Okay, so she looked like a double-decker London bus, but so what!

Max stood in the kitchen, admiring the sandwiches he'd placed neatly on a plate and waiting to make the tea, when Joey emerged.

Excitement skittered through him. It was a different kind of excitement from others he'd experienced, although most of that had been excitement arising from a hint—or even a real possibility—of danger.

This was personal excitement of a kind he'd never felt before. And given how horrified he'd been about the news that he'd fathered her baby—any baby—and the cynical voice in his head telling him he was mad, it was beyond weird. Right up until she'd gasped with the contraction, he'd been sure he could stay detached and make calm, clinical decisions about the future. Then suddenly the imminent arrival of *his* child had turned his world upside down.

He'd become a typical father-to-be—excited, panicky and scared. Involvement with the child he'd accidentally fathered was no longer an issue. This woman was about to have *his* baby, and given that whoever had been going to be with her for the birth was not available, he wanted desperately to be able to be there instead.

Who better? he asked himself. He *was* a doctor, his

training had included obstetrics, so being a birthing partner shouldn't be a problem.

He was pondering the best way to suggest it when she appeared from the bedroom, resplendent in a vivid red tracksuit that seemed to reflect its colour into her cheeks.

With her pale skin and dark, shining hair tumbling from its confining band, she looked beautiful—bountiful but beautiful.

'I don't know what to do,' she admitted. 'All I can remember from my obstetrics training is that women often go to hospital four or five times with false contractions, although—'

She stopped, gripping the table, sure what she was feeling couldn't possibly be false.

'Another one?' Max asked, reaching out to hold her hand.

She nodded then slowly relaxed.

'Fifty minutes apart,' he said, and Joey looked at him in amazement.

'Wrong, I had one in the bath. You timed them?'

He grinned at her.

'Well, I did learn a few things in medical school.' He smiled at her. 'And so must you.' He motioned to the open book on the table. 'So why do you have this book?'

To his surprise, she smiled back at him.

'If you remember, all we learned was from the doctor's perspective. We certainly didn't learn how to help the labouring woman—unless it was about pain relief or emergency procedures. I had intended going to the classes where you learn all the breathing stuff, but what with work and getting the nursery ready, I never got around to it.'

He thought for a moment.

'That stuff should be taught to medical students, shouldn't it? We should know what's happening to the woman, apart from how often her contractions are coming and how open her cervix is.'

'The book will tell us.' And Joey smiled again, the panic he'd seen in her eyes earlier easing as she spoke. 'That's if we have time to read the book.'

We? She was using the plural pronoun and it brought a riveting charge of excitement through Max's body, but before he could ask what it meant, Joey was speaking to him again.

'What do you think? Should I wait for another or just go to the hospital?'

Max felt a surge of pride that she was asking him, although, in truth, he had no idea of the answer. Surely they'd learned that much!

'Let's phone the hospital and see what they say.' He was inordinately proud of himself that he'd thought of such a sensible suggestion. And it must have been okay, for Joey perched on a stool, picked up one of the sandwiches and bit into it while she dialled an obviously well-known number.

He was surprised, given her tirade earlier, to hear how calmly she spoke, and he guessed that the contractions, on top of his unbelievable news, had just been too much for her. But she seemed back in control now, and ready to go through the final stages of what must have been a long, lonely pregnancy.

She was certainly something, this woman!

'So?' he asked, as she finished her call.

'Hospital when I'm ready but there's no rush unless the contractions start to get much closer,' she reported. 'I guess that means I'll have time to pack a bag—yes, I know it should have been done earlier—and maybe, on the way, call in at an all-night chemist for some nappies. People have given me heaps of clothes, and I've done a lot of research on disposable nappies and know what I want, it was just one of the hundred things I was going to do in the next couple of weeks. I'd sort of...' She sounded suddenly unsure. 'I'd sort of assumed...hoped...it might be late.'

Max had to smile, although he heard the panicky note back in her voice.

'Don't worry about nappies. Unless maternity hospitals have changed since I did my training, they have an endless supply, so you won't need your own until you get home.'

'Which could be tomorrow,' Joey told him. 'Women are lucky if they get to stay in overnight—Oh, damn!'

'What now?'

'I've bought a new car because the old one I've been driving doesn't have the secure places to attach capsules and seats. I was having the baby capsule fitted next week. Now I won't be able to bring the baby home!'

She'd bought a new car just to have a baby capsule securely fitted? The woman continued to amaze him, but she was sounding stressed again.

'Don't worry,' he said instead. 'I know this isn't how you'd planned things and you certainly didn't need the shock I landed on you, but now I'm here, I can help. I'm not working at the moment, just waiting on a couple of contract jobs that are coming up, so I can buy the nappies and fit the capsule. I can even, if you wouldn't mind, be your birthing partner. Just let me read the book. I'll do a speed read and you can tell me exactly what your friend was going to do.'

Joey stared at him. Was this man for real?

Had he just offered to support her through the birth of her child?

Most men would run a hundred miles—that's unless they were the father—

Which he was—or presumably was.

It was all too much, but right now the thought of going through her labour alone was terrifying.

'Do you mean that?'

'About fitting the capsule? Of course.'

'I don't mean that, I mean the being with me for the birth. Would you do it?'

He grinned and this time she *knew* the weird sensations in her body were nothing to do with impending childbirth.

Or the panic she was trying to suppress.

'Try and stop me,' he said, still grinning. 'You finish your sandwiches and I'll keep reading so I'll know how best to help you.'

It had to be shock—that, and the release of new hormones as her body got ready to give birth. Why else would she be not only agreeing to this man going through the event with her but even feeling appreciative towards him?

Thankful!

Grateful!

No, make that pathetically grateful.

Not that she'd tell him.

Night had fallen and the lights of the city twinkled and flickered beneath him as Max strode swiftly back down the terrace towards a private parking station Joey had described as 'you can't miss it.' He wasn't so sure, just as he wasn't certain he'd actually find the car whose keys he carried. 'It's a kind of silvery blue, or maybe a silvery green,' Joey had told him, 'and the capsule's still all wrapped up in the back seat. I did have the reg number, but the paper's in the car glove-box so that's no help.'

And this woman was going to raise *his* baby?

She probably wasn't nearly as daffy as she seemed. Shock could turn anyone a bit peculiar. He'd been angry at the clinic, *very* angry, but shock had certainly struck him as the hugely pregnant woman had walked through the door of the consulting room.

His 'that's *my* baby in there!' thought had definitely brought on shock.

Though the emotion that had followed—a surging, prideful sense of ownership—*that* had been the biggest shock.

Especially when he'd so recently confirmed in his head that children weren't for him.

It had to be a genetic thing, going back to caveman times—a tiny bit of cellular material that made a man protective of his child.

The key fob opened a silver—straight silver as far as he could tell—sedan with a wrapped baby capsule in the back seat, on the third floor of the parking station. The woman did love her stairs!

After easing back the seat and studying the unfamiliar controls, he drove back to the old building, pulling into one of two parking bays in what had once been a small front garden.

Joey was sitting on the front steps, a bag beside her, her head tilted to one side as she held the book she was reading to the light.

Could she really be as calm as she looked?

He walked towards her, holding out his hand to help her to her feet, but as she took it she must have felt some pain for her fingers tightened on his, gripping strongly, clinging to him until, with a deep sigh, she relaxed and released his hand, pushing herself to her feet.

'Contraction?' he asked, his own gut now tight with tension.

She smiled. 'A small one but definitely a contraction,' she said. 'This is good. Now it's started I'd like to get it over and done with.'

'Although…' she added, after a slight hesitation. She was looking into his face, and even in the light from a streetlamp outside the building he could read the worry in her eyes.

'There's something—no, there *could* be something— wrong,' she whispered, fear edging the words.

'With you?' Max asked, taking her hand again.

'With the baby.'

The words were little more than a sigh, then she straightened up, took a deep breath, and said, 'The last scan—as you can see, I'm huge and the scans showed polyhydramnios, which you probably remember just means lots of fluid. The baby wasn't cooperating with the scan so they couldn't see a problem, but there could be.'

Another pause before she added, 'I thought you should know.'

Max folded his arms around her, holding her as close as he could, and dug back through his memory—polyhydramnios was associated with Down's syndrome and possibly other congenital birth defects.

'You had other tests?' he asked, because that was the practical thing to say while inside he was wondering how well he'd cope if his child needed special help.

A warm feeling inside told him he'd be fine—just the words 'his child' brought on such a sense of achievement he knew he could conquer anything.

You've gone nuts, the cynic in his head muttered, *you do not need to be involved with this child,* but he barely heard the words.

'Of course, so it's nothing obvious,' she said.

'We'll manage,' he told her, and she stepped back and looked into his face.

'Oh, will *we*?' she said, although he was sure there was a smile in the words. 'Anyway, it might be nothing at all, so for now let's just get him or her out and take it from there.'

She was all practicality again, tucking the book into the pocket of her top while he helped her into the car. He had no idea of what the future might hold, or his place in it with this woman and the child, so for now all he could do was go with the flow. She'd handed him the car keys earlier, asking if he'd mind driving her to the hospital—'not that I can't drive, I just feel a bit spacey'—so she was offering him a certain level of trust.

It wasn't until he'd backed out onto the road again that he realised he had no idea where he was going.

'Across the river. I'm not so spacey I can't give directions,' she said, guessing his dilemma.

Before the directions began, a phone sounded, so he pulled to the kerb while Joey rummaged in her bag.

After the initial greeting, her end of the conversation wasn't hard to follow.

'Jacqui, calm down. Where are you? Where are your mum and dad? Will you let me call the ambulance?' She sighed as he heard shrill protests from the other end of the phone. 'Okay,' she said at last. 'Keep trying to contact your parents but I'll be there in ten minutes.'

'Change of plans,' she said as she closed the phone. 'One of my patients from this afternoon was hit by a bike on the way home from a friend's. She fifteen, a recovering anorexic as well as being a type one diabetic. She loathes doctors, loathes hospitals. It's taken me ages to get her trust. It sounds like she's damaged her shoulder but I'm more worried about her sugar level. She's home alone and she's terrified. I have to go.'

Max felt his draw drop in disbelief.

'Whoa! Hang on there a moment, lady! We're on our way to hospital for you to have a baby. You can't go dashing off to tend to other medical emergencies.'

'I don't have a choice. Jacqui trusts me and you have no idea how hard that was to achieve. I'm only in early labour. I'll be fine. But…but you don't have to come. I can drive.'

She didn't sound too sure about the 'I can drive' part, and the 'but' had been definitely scared.

'This is crazy,' Max told her. 'Right now you should be thinking about yourself—thinking about you as a patient, not you as a doctor. You've just had a contraction.'

'I know.' And this time he definitely heard fear. 'I want…what's best for my baby. You don't know how much. But, Max, I know she's desperate. If she's having a hypo…'

He gazed at her and she gazed back. Conflicting emotions were all over the place. She needed to be in hospital. He needed to get her there.

One fifteen-year-old, with diabetes…

'If the worst comes to worst, you're a doctor,' she said, trying to sound courageous. 'Surely you can remember how to deliver a baby.'

Oh, yeah?

Shock had blanked his mind of medical knowledge, but he knew it would come back to him. And of course he'd known the first contractions rarely meant anything, apart from the fact that labour had started. It was just that he'd prefer her to be in hospital where someone else would be responsible for the delivery.

'Let's go,' she said. 'It's not as if this baby is going to pop out any minute.'

Was he really sitting in a car, arguing with a woman in labour—a woman who, at some stage, would produce his baby?

It was beyond belief!

'Drive or get out,' she was saying now, although she hadn't opened her door, so obviously she was just testing him.

'I'll drive,' Max found himself growling, but he put the car into gear and indicated to pull away from the kerb. 'Just tell me where to go.'

Follow her directions, the calm, positive and in-control part of him suggested, so he ignored the panic fluttering through the rest of him, took a deep breath and drove the car where he was told to drive it.

Down off the terrace, around the edge of the city, along the broad river, then up to a grand house with a sweeping view.

'Are you sure about this?' Max asked worriedly. 'There has to be some other way.'

'Jacqui won't ask for help. She's so stubborn she's dangerous.'

'Stubborn! Tell me about stubborn,' Max snorted, but Joey was already clambering awkwardly out of the car. Should she have bought something higher and easier to get out of?

Not that she'd be pregnant much longer.

The door was unlocked. Joey knocked. No answer. She pushed and went inside. Jacqui was sitting in the drawing room, hands shaky, sweat on her brow.

'Joey...'

'Hey.' Joey started forward but Max was suddenly beside her, holding her back, then astonishingly pressing her to sit in one of the chairs. Great, Joey thought. What if her waters broke? What if...?

'Hi,' Max was saying to Jacqui, who was backing in alarm.

'Who...who are you?'

'I'm Dr McMillan's birthing partner,' he said, and sighed and knelt before the scared-looking kid. 'It's okay. Joey's in labour, but she's promised not to have the baby until you're okay. I'm a doctor, too, and while Joey's concentrating on baby, can I concentrate on you?'

The girl gave Joey an awed look. 'Really?'

'Really,' Max said. 'Jacqui, you look sweaty. Point me to the kitchen. Do you have juice?'

'I... Yes.'

'And where's your test kit?'

'In my backpack.'

'That arm's hurting?' She was cradling it, protecting it—from him?

'Y-yes.'

'Where are your parents?'

'My mum's out with friends. She's not answering the phone. Dad's at a meeting and he hates me disturbing him.'

'You won't be disturbing him, I will be,' Max said, giving Joey a quelling glance. 'Okay, Jacqui, let's get you sorted so Dr McMillan can get on with having her baby.'

He found the juice. He tested her blood sugar and insisted on more juice. He fashioned a support sling to hold her arm immobilised and then barked orders at her hapless dad on the end of the phone.

Then he waited, watching both Jacqui and Joey until Jacqui's dad got home. Compelling them both to sit still. To rest. No dramas on his patch.

By the time her father arrived, Joey had had two more contractions and Jacqui was so intrigued she'd almost forgotten about her own pain.

'You need to take your daughter to hospital,' Max told her father. 'She needs that shoulder x-rayed.'

'I won't go,' Jacqui said sullenly.

'See, we have a choice,' Max told her. 'Joey won't go to hospital until you do. This is nice white shag pile carpet. It's not exactly birth material. Our baby might come at any minute. The only way you can make Joey safe is for you to agree to be treated.'

'That's blackmail,' Jacqui gasped, and Max beamed.

'You have it in one.'

'Our baby?' Jacqui asked.

'Ours,' Max said, and headed back to Joey. He knelt and put his arm around her. 'Help me out here, Jacqui. Agree to get your arm x-rayed.'

'Please,' Joey added, as another contraction hit.

And there was no choice. With one eye on his daughter's arm, and another on his beautiful carpet, Jacqui's father turned dictatorial. They left and Max was able, finally, to usher his lady back into the car.

His lady? Why did it feel like that was the right description? She was so brave, he thought. What other woman would insist on putting the needs of an ill fifteen-year-old before her labour?

'You didn't have to say our baby!' she muttered at him as soon as they were out of earshot.

'It helped,' he explained. 'I have a niece about that age

and any hint of romance between adults is a huge deal. Not, of course, that's there's any hint of romance here, but she wouldn't know that. It got her distracted and she's getting an X-ray because of it. Good result.'

The explanation didn't do much good, to judge from Joey's frown as he helped her into the car.

'Does it matter, people knowing it's ours?' he asked as he climbed in beside her.

She turned to him, a puzzled look on her face.

'I guess—I really don't know. I feel so out of it somehow… Detached…'

'Spacey,' he provided, as her voice tailed away. 'And for someone who's admitted feeling spacey *and* who is having contractions, you need to turn off your phone, stop being a doctor and let yourself be looked after.'

'By…you?'

'By me,' he said grimly. He took her phone from the car console and tucked it in his jacket. 'I'm in charge—sort of—until we have a baby.'

CHAPTER FIVE

SHE TOLD HIM which way to turn to get back to the road along the river. She succumbed to silence.

Once again he got that feeling of fear. He wanted to pull over and read the book. What to do when the lady giving birth was frightened?

Distract her?

'You haven't really explained why you decided to have this baby,' he said.

'For David?'

'Is that a question?'

'No.' She shook her head and stared ahead for a bit. 'I guess…all I had was work. For so long…'

'Is that why you decided to have the baby? To give you something other than work to live for?'

The road was well lit so he could see the astonishment in her expression as she turned towards him.

'Of course not! I'd sort of promised David. I mean… he hadn't made me promise but I know he would want it. His parents quite desperately want a grandchild. Anyway, it'll enhance my work, having a child of my own, experiencing child-rearing, something that's been book-learning up to now.'

'So you're having this baby as a tool to make yourself a better paediatrician?'

He couldn't disguise his disbelief so it wasn't surprising she went all defensive on him.

'It's not like that at all!' she snapped, but there was an undertone of uncertainty beneath the words. 'And, anyway, it's none of your damn business.'

'Oh, yes, it is!' he retorted. 'That baby's mine as well, remember.'

'So you say, and, anyway, you've missed the turn. You should have turned to the right back there and onto the bridge.'

Shut up and drive, in other words, Max muttered to himself, but the conversation had disturbed him. He knew people had babies for all kinds of reasons, but shouldn't there be an element of love? The ex-husband was in the equation, he thought, but only just.

'If you go left now we can come at it from the other way.'

She sounded so forlorn as she gave the direction, Max regretted the entire conversation. Did it really matter why she was having the baby?

Wasn't it enough that she *was* having it, and soon?

'I *did* want to do it for David.' The whispered words made him ease his foot off the accelerator, aware there must be something she needed to say. 'But it's the love thing that held me back—still worries me. Loving the baby.'

She turned, her face pale in the streetlights.

'Loving someone makes you a hostage to fate.'

The words stabbed into his heart. She'd suffered the terrible pain of losing the man she'd loved and now feared the same pain should something happen to her baby.

So she told herself all the stuff about it being good for her career in the hope that...

That what?

She wouldn't love too hard?

Too deeply?

Too passionately?

'Now over the bridge, along beside the park, and up the hill.'

She was back to giving directions but was still subdued. Was she in pain?

His heart ached for her, and he reached out and rested his hand lightly on her knee.

She covered it with her own, and he drove up the hill towards the huge building. The hospital.

Was it inappropriate that as well as an enormous empathy for her, he felt excitement stirring in his gut?

'I'm not exactly an emergency,' she said as he pulled into the emergency bay.

'But you're not a "walk through the front door with the visitors" person either,' he told her firmly, parking the car and helping her out.

Accustomed to pregnant women appearing on the doorstep, an orderly was already wheeling a wheelchair towards them.

'I'd prefer to walk,' Joey said firmly, but when she turned back towards Max, there was anguish in her wide blue eyes.

Had he put it there with his unthinking words earlier?

Or was it apprehension about what lay ahead?

'You *will* come with me, won't you? Stay with me?'

Max swallowed hard. This was ridiculous. They weren't anywhere near the nitty-gritty part and here he was getting emotional. He, who'd been decidedly ambivalent about this baby business when he'd been hit with the startling information. Maybe occasional contact had been as far as he'd got in his head before he'd actually seen Joey and her huge belly.

'I'll just park the car and come and find you,' he assured her, then he stepped towards her, kissed her on the cheek, squeezed her shoulder, and added, 'Promise!'

A kiss on the cheek and a large warm hand on her shoulder—surely such simple gestures couldn't bring on a wave of wellbeing? No, put it down to endorphins. Didn't they kick in when contractions started? Speaking of contractions…

Joey leaned against the wall, wanting to bring out the book but sure it was too late to be reading it again. She remembered the wave—go up it then down, sigh and breathe, but in what order she couldn't remember.

Did it matter?

Just get through the pain.

She wanted Max!

She wanted someone, anyone, she told herself, not necessarily him.

The pain eased and she pondered her reaction as the orderly took her inside. She'd done her obstetrics training years ago at another maternity hospital across the river, and one of the things on her to-do list in the lead-up to the birth had been to visit the maternity ward of this particular hospital.

So much for plans!

Max was already there when the orderly wheeled her into what looked like a small but quite pleasant hotel room. A nurse greeted her, holding a clipboard that no doubt held all the details Joey had given the hospital when she'd made the booking. It was all so familiar, and yet so strange.

'Okay?' Max asked, and she nodded, then shook her head.

'I didn't look at the time. I should have looked at the time when I had those other contractions.'

'That's what I'm for, remember,' Max said, smiling at her. 'They're fairly regular.'

The nurse smiled at him before turning to Joey.

'You get yourself comfortable and I'll do a quick examination of you and the baby, then you can walk or sit or lie down, you can stand under the shower, or sit in a bath— whatever makes you feel relaxed.'

She lay on the bed for the examination, the pregnancy book dropping out of her pocket as she pulled up her top. Max grabbed it and sat down in a chair beside the bed, watching the nurse, taking note of the squiggles she was making on the chart.

'You've not had many contractions?' the nurse asked, when she'd checked the dilatation of Joey's cervix.

'Nine,' Max told her, counting them in his head.

'Well, you're doing well to be three centimetres dilated. Shouldn't be too long a job.'

'Does she think that's reassuring?' Joey demanded of Max when the young woman had left the room.

He smiled at her.

'In my experience, doctors make the worst patients,' he said.

'And what *is* your experience?' Joey asked, realising that not only would it pass the time to learn about this man but that she was actually interested.

'My basic skill set consists of tropical and emergency medicine mainly,' he said. 'But shouldn't we be reading the book rather than talking about me?'

'Bother the book. You climb snow-covered mountains yet you're into tropical medicine?'

'I've climbed mountains in Africa and South America too, but I was born in North Queensland, and although the most common of the tropical diseases spreading into Australia is dengue fever, other viruses and parasitic diseases are sneaking in. It's also useful for travel medicine, which is a growing field.' He hesitated. 'I have a job offer coming up later this year—a lecturing and research position at the Sunshine Coast University, and working in their travel clinic. I might...' He hesitated. 'I might even take it.'

'Giving people jabs before they go overseas?' Joey teased. 'That's tough stuff!'

'And finding out what's wrong with them when they return,' Max retorted. 'That's becoming my main interest—

working out how we can build a barrier of protection. People forget how easily something like the SARS virus could enter Australia and spread through the population.'

But he realised Joey had stopped listening, as he saw her face tighten and she reached for his hand.

'I think I'm better standing,' she muttered, and he helped her up, then he stood so she could lean on him as the pain gripped her.

Forget that she wanted conversation, *he* wanted to read the book. He wanted to know what to do to help her as much as he could, to ease her pain as the contractions ripped through her body.

He waited until she relaxed again, checked the time, then suggested she might like, as the nurse had suggested, to walk.

She nodded and strode towards the door, Max having to hurry to get there before her to open it and then slide his arm around her shoulders to give her support as she walked.

He held her close, liking her warmth, assuming she was comfortable with his closeness as she was nestling into him, clutching him when pain struck, accepting his support.

'Keep talking,' she'd ordered, and he obeyed, rambling on about the spread of new diseases, about the recent tests of a possible AIDS/HIV vaccine and its importance, speaking briefly of his work with emergency response units, while his mind was totally focussed on the woman who leaned on his arm.

Four passes up and down the corridor, nodding at another walking couple each time they passed, then Joey needed the bathroom, informed him she was perfectly capable of peeing by herself, and left him to flick hurriedly through the book.

'Look,' he said when she emerged, 'you can sit backwards on a chair and rest your belly and head like this— would that be comfortable?'

'Not right now!' she told him, her grasp tightening on

his hand once more while she leaned her head against the wall and rode the wave he'd been reading about. He rubbed her back, following advice he'd read and offering more.

'Sigh as the pain goes up, then breathe deeply at the top, then a big sigh at the end,' he told her, and she waited until the contraction had passed before she turned to glare at him.

'I think anyone who didn't sigh at the end would be out of her mind!'

He smiled at her reaction but was undeterred.

'You should rest in between. Sit down, lie down, whatever is best, that's why Fiona suggests the chair. I'll get the pillows, you might even doze.'

To his delight she actually settled on the chair, a pillow against her belly, another under her head on the top of the chair-back.

'Not bad,' she said, albeit grudgingly. 'Now talk!'

Max stood beside the chair, rubbing his hands in Joey's hair, massaging her scalp, her neck and then her back, and talking, talking, talking.

He edited a lot of what he was saying, as the years he'd spent working in Africa had revealed illnesses and diseases that had horrified even him. Not mentioning he was due to go back to Africa in a less than a month, as one of the medical personnel involved in the AIDS/HIV research, or the on-call ERU stuff he'd been doing since the rescue in the Himalayas.

Of course he couldn't commit himself to this baby— not with the life he led. What had he been talking about earlier? Where that stupid marriage idea had come from, he couldn't think.

But the child would be his, for all it was only accidentally so.

Could he *not* commit to it?

He talked on, massaging, walking with her, torn apart by his contrary thoughts, because as well as the child, now he'd met her. Could he walk away from this woman who'd come so unexpectedly into his life?

This very special woman...

At some stage night turned into day. Joey, her dark hair clinging in damp tendrils to her whitened cheeks, clung grimly to Max's hand, sipping at the ice he offered her, accepting his ministrations as he mopped the sweat from her face, soothing her with touch and words.

Her silence through the process staggered him. Apart from muffled groans, the occasional swear word and regular demands he talk to entertain her, she bore it all so stoically he had been suffering lumpy-throat syndrome for the last couple of hours.

'Do you want to catch the baby?'

Max was so fully engrossed in urging Joey to push he barely heard the midwife's words, let alone made sense of them, and when he did, he could only wonder.

He looked at Joey, saw her nod, and moved to stand beside the midwife, gazing in awe at the smear of dark hair on the crowning head, the shoulders turning as they slid out, then a tiny, slippery baby boy was in his hands, and he was trembling with the wonder of it.

The midwife took the baby, settling him gently on Joey's breast, her hands coming up to cradle the little scrap of humanity she'd carried for the last eight months.

'A boy,' she said softly, looking up at Max, her eyes as full of awe as his must be.

'Do you mind?'

She shook her head, tears now streaking down her cheeks.

He sat beside her, his arm around her shoulders, the two of them gazing in wonder and delight at the new arrival.

'You've a bit more to do yet, Mum,' the midwife said, 'but first we'll get Dad to clamp the cord.'

'Mum? Dad?' Joey mouthed at him, smiling in spite of

her exhaustion, but Max was beyond worrying about what the midwife called him. He was about to separate his baby from his mother, and a new little life would begin.

Checked, weighed, measured and with his mother cleaning up, Baby—

Baby what?

Joey was still in the bathroom when this occurred to Max.

Hospitals always called the baby by his or her surname but Baby what? McMillan or Winthrop? Obviously Joey would be thinking McMillan—

Did it matter?

He knew it shouldn't, but in his heart he knew it did. This was *his* baby.

The cynic who'd obviously been resting during the labour returned to mutter a dry, 'Oh, please!' but Max was beyond caring what the voice was saying.

This was *his* baby.

And just thinking it brought the doubts crowding back into his head.

Just how reliable could he be in the father stakes?

Worse than his own father?

Max hoped the squirmy feeling in his stomach was tiredness.

And the nurse was already writing Baby McMillan on the card that would slot into crib and on the identity bracelet the infant would wear in hospital.

Of course it didn't matter, Max told himself. The baby isn't going to know what he was called in hospital and with the baby's surname and Joey's the same, he wouldn't go to the wrong mother for his feeds.

Joey emerged from the bathroom, the dark circles under her eyes vivid against the paleness of her skin.

'You need to rest,' he said, and she found a smile.

'So must you,' she said. 'I guess it's been a kind of un-expected twenty-four hours for you.'

Unexpected?

Life-changing more like, but exhaustion had caught up with him and when she suggested that the bed was big enough for both of them to lie on, he took her up on it, set-tling on one side, thankful hospitals like this one now ca-tered to fathers as well as mothers in the birthing suites.

'I'll take him to the nursery where the paediatrician will check him out. The paediatrician is due in shortly,' the nurse told them. 'Once he's been, you can have the baby rooming in, probably as soon as you wake up.'

She wheeled the baby out and Joey rolled to face Max on the bed.

'I didn't thank you,' she said, reaching out to touch his shoulder. 'You were wonderful. I couldn't have done it without you.'

He took her hand and kissed it.

'Thank *you*,' he said, 'for allowing me to be part of his birth.'

And he held her hand between them on the bed and watched her eyes close as she drifted off to sleep. Four-teen hours of labour—she'd done so well he felt a pride in her that was really quite ridiculous, considering the fact that, although she'd just given birth to his son, he didn't know her at all.

Yet laying beside her on that bed seemed right—as if capricious fate had finally put him down in the place where he was meant to be...

She was sleeping deeply when he woke a couple of hours later, and he slid carefully off the bed and went out to the bathroom he'd discovered in the corridor some time dur-ing the night.

He looked a wreck. From what he could remember of the drive, the serviced apartment he was renting wasn't far away—across the river but probably within walking distance. He splashed water on his face and although he knew he should go back there, shower and shave and tidy himself up, he didn't want to leave the hospital.

Leave the baby.

Or Joey…

Which—and he had to agree with the cynical voice—was ridiculous.

He was telling himself to get moving when he remembered Joey's concern that there might be something wrong with the baby.

How could he have gone to sleep before the paediatrician had checked the baby out?

The nurse had given the tiny boy a good Apgar score, but the paediatrician?

Forget cleaning up. Max went in search of his son.

No sign of Baby McMillan in the nursery.

He asked the first uniformed person he found.

'He's in Special Care—nothing serious, but they've got him on oxygen for the moment. He could have inhaled a little meconium during the birth.'

'Can I see the paediatrician?' Max asked—yes, asked, although he'd have liked to have made the question more forceful.

'He's with the baby now. I'll take you through.'

She led Max into a kind of glassed-in alcove off the main nursery.

Not Intensive Care, then, was Max's first thought, checking out the area that was set up for special care, a big comfy chair set up beside each crib.

'Max Winthrop? What the hell are you going here? Last I heard you were scaling mountains in very inhospitable places.'

Bob Jenkins had trained with Max in North Queensland, and finding Bob in charge of the baby brought immediate relief, even though Max had no idea of Bob's ability as a paediatrician.

'He's mine,' he told Bob, 'and, yes, he's Baby McMillan but he's mine as well. Joey had a lot of fluid, and her obstetrician, who's off holidaying somewhere, was concerned during the pregnancy.'

'It's in the notes,' Bob told him. 'He's presenting okay, but I'm about to do an ultrasound just to make sure.'

Max looked at the tiny mite in what seemed like far too large a crib. He was wearing nothing but a very small nappy—he must tell Joey—and had wires and tubes attached all over him. Nothing Max hadn't seen before, but on a very small baby the electrodes to measure his heart rate and breathing looked enormous while the monitor strapped to his foot was probably for blood oxygen levels, not a shackle to prevent his escape.

The size of him, the tubes and wires, caused pain in Max's heart and it was hard to tell himself he would feel for any newborn in the same situation.

'I'll go and see if his mother is awake and come back,' he told Bob, only too aware there'd have been no mention of him in the notes Bob had read, and his old friend must have a dozen questions—not to mention be in an ethical dilemma in case Max had no rights at all where Baby McMillan was concerned.

Joey was still sleeping, looking so peaceful, so relaxed, a little smile on her lips as if her dreams were sweet. He should let her be. She'd need to be as strong as possible in case she had to handle any bad news.

He hit his head with the palm of his hand, telling himself to get with it. He'd missed more nights' sleep than he could count, so why was he getting uptight?

Because something about this woman had cast a spell on him?

Of course not, it was because this was not only a defenceless baby, but it was *his* defenceless baby, that's why.

Good grief, what was he going to be like when the kid went to school for the first time?

And *that* thought made him pause!

Was he really considering being a full-time, hands-on father?

Would that be possible?

Or would giving up all the work he loved doing, make him as unhappy and dissatisfied as his father had been?

Why had he told Joey about the job offer at the Sunshine Coast? He had no intention of taking it—did he?

He had no answer to any of the questions, just an immediate need to be with the baby while the scan was done.

And Joey should be there as well.

He sat on the bed beside her and gently shook her shoulder, quietly saying her name.

Her eyes opened, hazy at first, looking up at him, smiling.

His stomach somersaulted, and his heart leapt about like a startled deer. Even when his mind should be fully focussed on the baby.

Of course he'd be a hopeless failure as a father.

'Max?'

Concern had wiped away the smile and as she struggled to sit up, he found some common sense and helped her, holding her around the shoulders.

'It's okay,' he assured her, 'but the paediatrician's with the baby now and I thought you'd like to be there while they checked him out. They're doing an ultrasound.'

She all but leapt off the bed.

'It's okay—he's waiting. I'll take you there.'

He put his arm around her and when she didn't seem to mind, he left it there, guiding her back to where the portable ultrasound machine was set up beside the crib—the screen of its laptop providing the image.

'Just in time,' Bob said.

He greeted Joey, the two of them recalling the times they'd met before, exchanging courtesies.

'You'll know all this,' he said to Joey, 'but I'll run through it for the bloke you're with, who's more into weird diseases than neonatal problems.'

Joey nodded, but she remained pressed against Max's side, showing no objection to his arm around her shoulders.

If anything, she was pressing closer.

'Do you remember any of your neonatal paediatrics?' Bob was asking him. 'See here!'

He pointed to what looked like two small white balloons—one bigger than the other—in the baby's abdomen.

'Double bubble,' Joey breathed.

'A sure sign of duodenal atresia,' Bob confirmed.

Joey reached out to touch the baby, and Max could feel the quiver of fear running through her.

'But it's easily fixed?' he said to Bob, possibly too forcefully but wanting to offer Joey *some* comfort, while lessons learned long ago came rushing back into his brain.

Blocked duodenum—the little tube leading out of the stomach. He could even remember the picture in the neonatal textbook.

'Could it be indicative of other problems?' Max asked, fear for the child gripping his gut and accelerating *his* heartbeat now. 'Heart defects?'

'I've checked his heart as it's sometimes associated with congenital heart defects and I've taken blood for further tests, but I'd say it was just an anomaly during his development—the solid tube inside the foetus early on just didn't quite open.'

'It happens,' Joey said quietly, and he could feel that she'd relaxed, just a little, now she knew it wasn't something worse.

'It happens,' she repeated, leaning into Max but with her eyes still on the baby.

Just like accidents in IVF labs, Max thought. Exceedingly rare but not unknown.

'And what do we do about it?' Max asked, pretending to be very grown-up and practical about this, although inside he was a mess. 'Operate?'

It was the utter helplessness of the tiny infant that had clutched at his heart and had made Bob's matter-of-fact pronouncements so hurtful. And Joey, who would know exactly what was involved, must be feeling a million times worse.

'Yes, he'll need an op. First we'll get him stable, IV feeds, put a tube down to drain his stomach, then surgery. It's quite simple. The bloke I'd use—you'd know Prentice, Joey—does it through the navel. Once in he makes two tiny incisions through the duodenum, joins up the ends either side of the blockage and you're done.'

Max stared at the man who'd been quite a close friend all through university and wondered how he could be so casual—so laid back—about an operation on a newborn baby.

Bob was talking to Joey, explaining the expected time frame for the op, but Max's attention was all on the baby.

How could anyone operate on such a tiny infant?

Of course, he knew it happened all the time, particularly for babies born with congenital heart defects, but *his* baby?

'You and Max...' he heard Bob say, and their two names, linked like that, made it sound as if they were established partners.

But Joey and he *were* partners—in the baby if nothing else. His sudden realisation of this was a bit like an out-of-body experience he'd heard people describe, although those people were usually seriously ill or had been hit on the head. His hit had been to the heart.

Whatever—the out-of-body feeling didn't seem to be going away. He was lodged in a parallel universe where Joey and the baby had become priorities in his life.

Just for the moment, of course...

* * *

Bob had departed to organise the surgeon, and Max helped Joey into the chair beside the crib.

'I want to hold him,' she said, her voice still shaky from the news of the operation.

'I'll get a nurse to keep the tubes and wires untangled. Just sit for a minute.'

But before he could depart she grabbed his hand and he had to lean down close to her to hear the tremulous words that faltered from her lips.

'I couldn't have done it without you—though how any man could go through that with a stranger I've no idea. You were wonderful!'

And she smiled, the kind of smile that made it impossible not to drop a kiss on those tempting pink lips—a kiss that somehow deepened, until it was like a fine high-tensile wire holding them together, bonding them in something even bigger than the baby, although he was most definitely part of it.

'Weird, huh?' she said as they broke apart.

'Beyond weird,' he agreed, though he didn't share his parallel universe theory. Instead, he went to find a nurse to help settle the baby in Joey's arms.

It took only seconds to get the little one sorted, with the tubes and wires carefully arranged so nothing snagged.

Max sat on the arm of the chair and touched his son's stubby excuse for a nose.

'This surgeon, you know him?' he asked, as Joey examined the tiny ears, the perfect toenails, taking in the miracle that she'd produced.

Wide blue eyes looked up at him, fear beating in the air once again.

'He's fine—terrific—but, oh, Max, he's so tiny—the baby, not the surgeon.'

Joey held the baby close to her breast, reminding herself she'd known this might be the case and that duodenal atresia was one of the most common of problems in newborn babies.

But how could someone operate on this tiny mortal?

Her tiny mortal!

She tightened her arms around him, careful not to squash but wanting to hold him close forever. Max was saying soothing things but she barely heard, all her energy concentrated on the baby as if by will alone she could keep him safe—make him well.

Hearing but not listening, she explored her baby, touching the downy cheek, running her fingers over the soft hair on his head—dark hair that she knew he could well lose. David had been fair and she'd pictured his baby as fair like him—but this wasn't David's baby. And that was a whole other story.

Right now Max Winthrop's presence was a very reassuring bulk on the arm of the chair beside her. Although he'd been wonderful through the night, he'd told her enough that she knew he had wanderlust. He might want to be involved with his baby, but how much could she expect from him?

How much did she want from him?

A healthy baby was one thing…

She had too many questions and no answers at all!

'Look, I can stick around for a while so let's just keep going an hour at a time, then a day, and perhaps a week, and take it all as it comes,' he said, slipping an arm that she found immensely comforting around her shoulders.

'Did you learn to read minds in some ashram in India?' she asked, letting her cheek rest against his hip. She pulled the little cap back over the baby's hair, then looked up at his father. 'You answered my thoughts.'

He grinned at her.

'Not that hard when the same things are running amok in my head as well. It just seems to me that we take, well, baby steps, I suppose.'

The grin turned into a smile, a soft, gentle smile that somehow made her think everything would be all right.

Possibly forever!

How ridiculous! She didn't know the man; for all he was the father of her baby.

Which reminded her...

'Do you want to hold him?'

He reached down and slid his little finger into the palm of a tiny hand.

'No, he looks so peaceful lying there, I'm content to watch and wonder.'

'I wasn't really listening. Did Bob say when they'll operate?' she asked, looking up at him—seeing the wonder he spoke of in his eyes, feeling warmth flood her veins again as those eyes smiled at her.

Or had she imagined the smile? Because when he spoke he was all business.

'He'll contact the surgeon who'll come to see him, then talk to us.' He paused, then said quietly, 'Do you mind too much about the "us"? When I came to see you, I didn't envisage this happening, but now—well—do you mind that I want to be involved in all the discussion about the little fellow's health?'

Joey didn't have to think about it.

'I'm glad there's an "us,"' she answered honestly. 'I find the thought of him needing an operation very scary so I'm glad I'm not alone. I've got friends, of course, and they'll be wonderfully supportive when they know he has a problem, but it's not the same, is it? Because he's not *their* baby.'

'And he *is* ours,' Max agreed, tightening his grip on her shoulder. 'As I said before, we'll work it out.'

CHAPTER SIX

A NURSE APPEARED, needing to do a check, and they returned the baby to the crib.

'You can stay there, sit in the chair, and touch him as much as you like,' the nurse told them. 'Dr Prentice, the surgeon, will be here soon.'

'I'll stay,' Joey said, and found herself hoping Max would say the same, although he must be tired. But she would like him here when the surgeon came. Mike Prentice was an excellent neonatal surgeon. She'd worked under him during her training so she didn't really need to worry, but she would like Max to be there.

'I don't even know where you live.' The words came out as an accusation and she tried to make amends. 'I was thinking you'd probably like a shower and a shave, some clean clothes. If it's not too far, I could text you when the surgeon comes.'

'I'll stay unshaven and hopefully not too hard on the nose until after he's been, but to answer your question, I'm temporarily in a serviced apartment across the river. My family is all in North Queensland. They're a stay-put lot and think of me as some kind of changeling because of my wanderings. Oh, hell!'

The 'oh hell' had sounded a bit desperate and as he didn't enlarge on it, Joey had to ask.

'Oh, hell?' she prompted.

He was frowning now, looking really concerned.

'It can't be that bad,' she said.

'Oh, no? Although he doesn't know it yet, this poor little bloke has myriad relations—grandparent, aunts, uncles, cousins, all of whom will think he's partly theirs and want to shower him with gifts, cluck over every detail of his birth, probably cry about the operation and generally want to be very much part of his life. What on earth am I going to tell them about him?'

'Maybe the truth?' Joey suggested, smiling at his obvious discomfort but excited at the same time that her baby would have a family.

She'd have a family?

Don't be ridiculous!

'Tell them I'd forgotten I'd stored away some sperm, mainly because my then fiancée that none of them liked in the first place insisted on it, and then you got it by mistake and this is the baby? Who's going to believe that?'

'Not very many people,' Joey agreed, 'but it *is* the truth. Although you hadn't told me the bit about the fiancée insisting before!'

She hesitated then knew she had to ask.

'Why didn't they like the fiancée? Or fiancées, plural.'

His turn to hesitate, and when he answered she suspected it wasn't the truth—or the whole truth.

'Only boy with three older sisters,' he said, glibly enough. 'No one was ever really going to be good enough for me.'

'Hmm,' Joey said, and let it rest, actually quite admiring of Max Winthrop that he wouldn't put his ex-fiancées down. Although she did want to ask what his sisters had thought of the second fiancée—the one of the Dear John text.

'Tell me about Joey McMillan,' he said, and she was glad she hadn't asked as he obviously wanted to get right away from the fiancée subject.

'Nothing much to tell,' she said. 'You've seen where I grew up, both parents doctors, grandparents before them the same, so both generations only had one child—too busy for more, I guess.'

She stopped, wondering how different life would have been if she'd had a sister to talk to, to share secrets with, or a brother to tease or be teased by. There'd been times she'd hated being an only child, although she'd always known she'd been loved.

It certainly would have helped when—

She stopped. Why tell him?

Why not?

'My parents and grandparents were in Thailand, celebrating Mum and Dad's fortieth wedding anniversary, and were out on a small boat when the tsunami hit.'

She'd told the story so many times it grew shorter and less emotional with each retelling. A flat sentence that hid such a wealth of horror she rarely allowed herself to think about it.

But Max obviously knew something of horror, for he put his arm around her shoulders again and drew her close to his side, trailing a hand ever so softly over her hair.

'There is no remedy for the pain of such loss,' he said quietly, 'or words that help. I cannot imagine what inner strength you must possess to have kept going after that.'

No wonder she thought of people she loved being hostages to fate!

No wonder she was afraid of loving her baby too much, when everyone else she'd loved had been snatched away from her.

He'd been undergoing treatment when the tsunami had devastated parts of Thailand and Indonesia, so Joey must have lost her family not long after David's death.

'You must have thought you were cursed.'

She tilted her head back to look up at him.

'I was certain of it. I was a total mess. In fact, young Jacqui we called in to see on the way to the hospital was my saviour. I was doing a stint at the kids' hospital, and I came across her as a patient. She'd recently been diagnosed with type one diabetes and was determined that there was no way she, or anyone else, was going to stick needles in her body every day. She was such a fighter, I felt ashamed of my own weakness, my self-pity, and convincing her that the treatment would be worthwhile—that she could turn into the artist she dreams of being—not only got me through that time but made me decide to specialise in paediatrics.'

'And she's become special to you now.'

It was a statement, not a question, and Joey knew that this man understood.

But thinking about Jacqui was better than dwelling in the past.

'She has. Especially when she became one of my first private patients when I started practising. Of course, there are more problems now she's a teenager because the chronic illness exacerbates all the normal behavioural changes in puberty. She's fought anorexia. Type one diabetes is so hard for adolescents to handle—there's a constant focus on food, which creates more problems. That's why I was worried about the effect of stress on her last night.'

'I can understand that. But what so-called normal behavioural changes would it affect?'

Joey smiled at him.

'Challenging authority is the easy one—how better to challenge your parents and those in charge than by not balancing your insulin, which is unbalanced enough anyway with growth hormones and sex steroids running rampant in their bodies?'

'Causing?'

He'd probably guessed she needed to be very careful to increase insulin doses to keep her blood glucose in control. 'Then there's all the outward adolescent stuff. If the girl with pink and purple spots on her skin becomes popular then they all want pink and purple spots. Part of being an adolescent is fitting in with the mob so no one notices all the strange stuff going on inside you. Kids with diabetes are different from the start, so it's only natural they suffer more from the bad things of adolescence—depression, anxiety, low self-esteem, and weight issues.'

Joey sighed.

'It was a really bad time to be having a baby,' she said, stroking the baby in question with feather-light fingers. 'As far as Jacqui is concerned.'

'She'll get through it,' Max assured her.

'You don't know that,' Joey retorted, wondering how she'd reached the stage of chatting so easily to this man— sharing her pain and her concerns with him. Not to mention sitting there with his arm around her.

'I think I do,' he said, and she glanced up to see him smile at her. 'I'm pretty sure that young girl would have taken you for a role model and seen your strength *and* learned from it.'

Still smiling, he teased some hair off her face, tucking it back behind her ear in a gesture that, for a moment, made her heart stop.

'Now, what we need in this place are positive vibes, so get with the programme. Positivity for Jacqui and positivity for this baby.'

He stopped rather abruptly and his smile had changed to a slight frown.

'He needs a name. Were you going to call him David? I don't mind at all if you do, it's a good strong name—'

'You don't mind at all if I do?' Joey repeated, and knew she sounded shell-shocked, because she'd been about to demand just why the hell he should mind when the reality of the situation struck her anew.

'Oh, heavens, of course, he's your baby too,' she muttered, more to herself than to him.

'I did think we'd established that, and the clinic was

quite certain the mistake had been made. But we can get Bob to do a DNA just to be sure,' Max told her, and felt a shudder run through her body.

She shook her head, and gave a gulp that could well have been a swallowed sob so he had to tighten his grip on her again and make noises he hoped were soothing.

'I don't think I could bear to know he belongs to some stranger,' she whispered, 'but, of course, you'll want to know.'

Feeling her distress, knowing it was partly the hormonal surge that would have accompanied the birth, he still didn't want her fretting. He put his hand under her chin and tilted her face so she was looking up at him again.

'Believe me,' he said, 'I don't need to have DNA proof. I know he's mine. I caught him, remember. He smiled at me and did a "Hi, Dad" kind of wink.'

Then, because she'd tasted so sweet the first time, he bent and kissed the full, pink lips, softly parted, not quite believing his words but definitely more relaxed.

She pulled away, although not immediately, staring up at him, definitely more surprised than disgusted, shocked or horrified. Which, of course, prompted the earthier side of him to want to do it again.

He *did* refrain. And to distract himself from his other thoughts, he returned to the subject he'd begun earlier.

'So, with that established, what about a name?'

Her turn to smile and he found he really liked it when she smiled—probably that earthy bit of him again!

'I've been trying to think of names for the last six months but for some reason all I could come up with was Caspar. And then I wasn't sure whether to spell it with a C or a K and, really, it's not a sensible name at all. He'd probably be teased at school.'

Caspar?

'And Casparina for a girl?' he teased, and saw colour rise in her cheeks.

'I know it's stupid, but pregnancy brain is a very strange phenomenon, and once something is lodged there, nothing will shift it.'

She studied the infant she'd continued to stroke.

'The problem is, you think once they pop out—now, *that's* an euphemism—you'll find a name that really suits them—that they'll look like a Bill, or Joe, or Sam, or whatever. But, in fact, they just look like babies.'

'Joe's probably out, because you'd have two of them in the house. But I like short, no-nonsense names if you want my opinion.'

'Tom? Sam? What about Elliot?'

'Elliot? You don't like short, no-nonsense names, then.'

It was easy banter, but underneath Max felt a thread of something—something that felt very like the careful, tiptoed steps of the early stages of a relationship. It only happened between a man and a woman when some intangible link was triggered between them, then conversations and even silences all had some other meaning—like a dance where you had to get the steps right before you could twirl and whirl in each other's arms.

It had started in the waiting room—this connection that couldn't be explained—then had strengthened as he'd held her, talking and encouraging her, breathing with her, through her labour.

'Harry's nice,' she said, and Max forgot his fantasies about relationships and looked down at his son.

'He *does* look like a Harry. It's good when he's little and a strong name for a man.'

He slipped off the chair and knelt closer to the crib, close to Joey's legs, and studied the baby.

'You'd like to be a Harry?' he asked, touching the soft cheek. Then he turned to look up at Joey. 'It's Harry, then?' he asked, as Bob appeared, leading a white-coated man behind him.

'Bit late to be proposing to her, isn't it?' Bob said, as Max clambered to his feet.

'You'll keep,' he said to Bob, and turned to introduce himself to the stranger.

The surgeon greeted Joey with a kiss on her cheek and a quick squeeze of her shoulder.

'Sorry we had to meet again under these circumstances, my dear,' he said, 'but you know the little fellow will be fine, don't you?'

He took them into an office off the outer corridor, sat them down, and quickly sketched what he would be doing on a whiteboard.

'All this will be familiar to you, Joey, but I like to run through it anyway. I'll also give you a link to a video of it you can watch if you want to,' he said. 'My secretary will get all the permission papers to you for signatures.' He looked at Max then back at Joey, adding, a little hesitantly, 'I understand just yours is needed, Joey.'

He'd made it a question, and Joey nodded, but as she was clinging tightly to his, Max's, hand, he didn't mind at all.

'I'll probably wait a full day, two if I have to,' the surgeon continued. 'I need to check his cardiac and pulmonary function and make sure his fluid and electrolyte balances are good. Because it's a laparoscopic repair, he should be out of hospital in about a fortnight. You can stay here with him, Joey, although they might take your bed in a day or so, and you'd be camping in the chair. Hospitals! There's good accommodation in a hotel across the road if that happens. It might also suit your partner if he wants to be close.'

'It all seems so—so ordinary,' Joey said, when Bob was showing the surgeon out, and they sat on in the small room.

'I suppose, to him, it is,' Max told her. 'Something to remember, I guess, with all our patients. While we might see a dozen cases of atypical TB in a month, for our patient, he's the only one who has it.'

Joey smiled, and he felt a little tug of pleasure that he could make her smile.

'Actually, I've never seen one case of atypical TB,' she said, 'let alone a dozen in a month, but I get the gist of what you're saying. The problem is far more special to the patient than it is to the professional.'

Bob returned at that moment and repeated most of what the surgeon had said.

'If the baby is up to it, he'll do the op tomorrow,' Bob added. 'He has to check if he can get a theatre and what else he has on. The sooner the better as the orogastric tube the little fellow has in can irritate the membranes of the oesophagus and stomach. Someone will let you know.'

'The sooner the better for me, too,' Joey said as they left the room. 'I know the man is a genius with neonates, and all will be well—'

'But you want it over with,' Max finished for her. 'Me too.'

He walked her back to the nursery then knew he had to go back to his apartment and clean up, pack his toiletries and some spare clothes and find a room in this nearby hotel. His apartment might be within walking distance but he didn't want to be that far away from the baby.

Or Joey.

Joey felt his departure like a physical loss. She'd met the man less than twenty-four hours ago, yet already she felt as if he was part of her.

Because they'd shared her hours of labour?

Because he'd been there for her through it all, and helped her with his chat, and jokes and determined practicality?

Or because she'd seen the tears in his eyes as he'd held his newborn son?

Was there something very special about this man, or was it just her out-of-balance hormones making her think such a thing?

She sighed and prodded gently at Harry's free foot, touching each toe in turn.

'I think he's a very nice man, your dad,' she told the sleeping child.

'And you've just discovered this?' a nurse asked, as she came from behind to do her regular check on Harry.

'Well, yes,' Joey replied, and she smiled to herself, because there was something a bit special about this whole thing, a feeling she had that her life was going to change, and not just because of Harry.

She brought up an image of Max in her head and studied his tall, rangy form, the red-brown hair, the clear green eyes, the lines on his face, fanning out from his eyes, curving on his cheeks to show he smiled and laughed a lot. Fond of his family from the way he spoke. Adventurous—was that good?

She sighed and, as the nurse was gone, told Harry that she thought he'd like him. 'I think he'll make a super dad,' she assured her son, then the logistics of it all struck her.

There was something about Max that suggested he wouldn't be content to be a part-time parent, but from what he'd told her of his lifestyle, how could he be anything else?

Yet he'd suggested marriage, or had she dreamed that during her labour?

Would it work?

Could it work?

The apartment had three bedrooms—

What on earth was she thinking? No way he could have been serious! And if he had been, then he was crazy. Not husband material, as two fiancées had already discovered.

He could be off to Africa anyway—she was sure she remembered that. He'd mentioned a job in Australia, but she'd heard the lack of enthusiasm. So he'd be gone. And wouldn't a part-time father for Harry be worse than no father at all?

What's more, given that even thinking of the man could

produce in her body little physical niggles that obviously weren't contractions as she was no longer pregnant, the idea of him in a bedroom close to hers was—

Disquieting?

Or exciting?

And why was the bedroom idea lingering?

Get over it, she told herself. Just because he was kind enough to suffer through your labour with you it doesn't mean he wants to go to bed with you.

But then he returned!

She'd been dozing in the chair, sensed a presence, opened her eyes and there he was.

Her heart gave a little skip as she took in the smiling, freshly shaven face, the dull green T-shirt that read 'Dads-R-Us', and his long, lean legs encased in jeans that would almost certainly show a very tidy butt.

'Where did you get it?' she demanded, pointing at the T-shirt.

'Got one for you, too,' he said. 'There was a market at Southbank with a stall that printed them right there, so I ordered one for each of us and picked them up on the walk back.'

He handed her a package wrapped in tissue, and she pulled out the T-shirt—a pretty dark blue-green colour, 'Mums-R-Us' printed in a very dark blue.

'And this,' he added, dropping another package in her lap.

The tiny T-shirt read, 'I belong to Joey and Max', and for some reason the wording, or perhaps the size of the garment, or possibly just hormones, brought tears to Joey's eyes.

'They're wonderful,' she told him.

Then, probably because he'd seen the tears, he leaned down and kissed her.

A soft and gentle kiss—a 'don't cry' kiss most probably, although it felt like a real kiss from what she could remember of real kisses.

And because it felt like a real kiss, it sneaked into hidden places in her body and warmed some of the bits of her she'd thought had died with David, and pulsed into her heart so it beat a little faster and sent blood to colour her cheeks.

'Thank you,' she said, and hoped he'd take it as a thank-you for the T-shirts when it was really a thank-you for making her feel alive again, making her feel like a woman.

He really shouldn't be kissing her. He knew it was just a surfeit of emotion clanging away inside him that had prompted him to do it. That, and the slight sheen of tears in the wide blue eyes...

And it was all very well wearing silly T-shirts and walking around with his chest puffed out because he had a child, but, really, what did it mean?

Joey was right.

Harry was *her* baby, for all he, Max, had been the first to hold him.

And, realistically, how could he fit a child into his life?

The shock of finding out, first about the pregnancy mistake then being catapulted into participation in the birth, had stopped the rational functioning of his brain.

But Harry *was* his child.

How could he not be involved in his life?

The same arguments rattled back and forth in his head, anchored by some conviction that this child deserved two parents, and for all his doubts he might just have to step up to the plate and be the dad Harry deserved.

'Are you okay?'

Joey was beside him in the wide passage outside the nursery, frowning slightly as she studied him slumped against the wall.

'Tired,' he said, and knew it was true. He might be showered and shaven but he'd had very little sleep. Of course he couldn't think straight.

'Go back to wherever you're staying and sleep,' Joey told him, chiming in with his own thoughts. 'Take the car.'

She rested her hand on his forearm and looked into his eyes.

'I couldn't have got through all this without you,' she said quietly, 'but I'm okay now. Don't feel you have to hang around for my sake. We'll be fine, Harry and me.'

He studied the face turned up towards him, and knew she spoke the truth, but the twist in his gut told him there was more to this than getting her through the birth of the child—

Their child!

It was the 'their' bit that was the problem.

Or would be if he let it.

'I *will* go back to the apartment and have a sleep,' he told her, and stopped himself before he said another word, before he made commitments, or hurt her by not making commitments.

He'd sleep and think about it all later.

Much later.

He put his hand over the smaller one that still rested on his arm and offered what he knew full well would be a very strained smile.

'Good night,' he murmured, holding himself back from the kiss that seemed to hover in the air between them.

Joey watched him stride down the corridor, in long, swift steps—like a man escaping.

She made her way back to her room, trying to remember the snippets of information about his life that he'd shared with her during her labour. Travel, always travel, as far as she could recall, although he'd probably only told her the interesting bits to keep her mind off what was going on with her body.

One thing she did recall was a commitment he had to

a project in Zambia—education and research into ways to protect healthy men and women—something that might slow the scourge that was decimating populations in developing countries.

And that, if she remembered rightly, was coming up fairly soon.

She plumped down on her bed.

'And why should that matter?' she asked herself, just as a nurse appeared in the doorway.

'Talking to yourself?' the cheery young man enquired.

Joey grinned at him.

'If I had the baby here, I could have pretended I was talking to him,' she said.

'Ah, but you don't,' he said. 'But not to worry, I do it all the time.'

He ran the checks he had to do, chatting all the time, asking about the baby, approving Harry as a name, assuring her Dr Prentice was the best neonatal surgeon in the city—easy, uncomplicated company for a few minutes.

Company!

She dug in the bag she'd packed so hurriedly the night before and found her mobile, turned it on to a welter of messages. All the friends who'd been keeping an eye on her through her pregnancy seemed to have phoned, most of them more than once, but it was Meryl's number that caught her attention.

Meryl, who'd last seen her going off with a total stranger.

Only he didn't feel like a stranger.

Cursing herself for even thinking such a thing, she called Meryl, who had already phoned the hospital and heard the news of Harry's early arrival.

'I thought I'd try them before the police,' Meryl joked. 'You never know what shock might do.'

She was so calm and sensible Joey talked to her for nearly an hour, telling her about Harry's problem, the surgery he'd need, keeping Max Winthrop's presence throughout her labour not exactly secret but unmentioned.

'I'll come up and see you both this evening,' Meryl said. 'Can I bring you anything? Do you want me to collect anything from your place?'

Joey assured her she had everything she needed, but thinking of the phone messages that needed to be dealt with she added, 'But if you wouldn't mind letting a few people know I'm here and fine. You have the list of people to contact. If you could just call Kirstie and Lissa, the word will soon spread.'

'And do I mention Max Winthrop?' Meryl asked.

'No. It's too complicated right now, isn't it?'

But Meryl didn't answer the question—not beyond a rather dubious 'Hmm' noise.

'Hmm doesn't help,' Joey muttered to herself when she'd cut the connection, although she realised now exactly why she'd asked Meryl to call her friends. That way, she wouldn't get caught into conversation about the actual labour and have to tell lies—or at least avoid the truth.

But how could she talk about Max's eruption into her life when she didn't know how she felt about it herself?

Perhaps she should stop thinking of the man and think of Harry. He would definitely benefit from having a dad.

She looked at the T-shirt she'd dropped on the bed and smiled.

A dad with a sense of humour…

His face popped up in her head and she felt a curl of excitement deep inside.

No, no, no, no, no, no, no! She *had* to stop thinking this way. She had to be cool, calm and sensible—had to think the thing through.

How could she, though, not knowing what Max was thinking about the future? About his involvement?

The getting-married thing had just been silly, a reaction

to all that was going on. Words spoken out of the confusion of shock.

She blinked away some sudden moisture from her eyes and told herself it was hormonal, this wistful feeling that had sneaked up on her.

You couldn't go marrying a total stranger just because you'd had his child!

Could you?

To divert her mind from unanswerable thoughts, she went back through her messages, found one from the IVF clinic telling her they'd been unable to contact her and had sent her an email.

Her fingers trembled as she opened the email. It was stupid but she suspected the trembling was more to do with the thought of finding out—at this stage—that Max wasn't the father!

How stupid! It would be good news!

But all the email did was confirm what Max had told her. It was full of apologies and excuses, and they were devastated for her and could she call at her earliest convenience.

So!

Well, if you thought about it, the father of her baby wasn't really a stranger.

A marriage of convenience?

Could it work?

Are you nuts?

CHAPTER SEVEN

MAX WOKE AT midnight, confused at first about where he was, until the tumultuous events of the previous twenty-four hours came flooding back to him.

Midnight!

Was Joey sleeping, or would be she sitting by Harry's crib, talking to him, touching his skin, worrying?

Maybe she *was* asleep, and he could roll over and go back to sleep himself.

But if she was sitting there—if she was too anxious and concerned to leave the baby—then shouldn't he, as Harry's father, do his bit?

Which brought him back to the father thing again.

He slid out of bed, showered and dressed, not in the new T-shirt but in a sober, check, buttons-up-the-front shirt that made him look responsible and trustworthy. A good kind of father for a kid to have.

Closing his mind to his doubts, because the one thing he knew right now was that Joey needed support, he made his way out into the night-dark streets, crossing the river on the pedestrian bridge, striding swiftly through the parklands, reaching the hospital a little after one.

He collected a cup of coffee from a machine, knowing it would probably taste terrible, and headed for the nursery.

Harry was still in the special care unit, but there was no sign of Joey.

Pleased that she must be getting some much-needed rest, he sank into the comfortable armchair beside Harry's crib and watched the baby sleep.

It took him at least three seconds to realise this was *not* a good idea. Not if he didn't intend staying involved with the child.

He knew it was totally ridiculous but he felt a connection to the baby, as if invisible strings stretched between them.

This was *his* child!

He reached out and let his hand rest against the warm skin of Harry's arm, and sat, content to be there, not thinking, just accepting, knowing a multitude of huge decisions and difficult arrangements lay ahead, but right now not caring about the future.

This was now and he was here, with his son—the only place on earth he wanted to be.

Joey woke with a start, unable to believe she'd slept through most of the night. She'd returned to her room to have a shower, eat some dinner, and talk to Meryl, but she'd had every intention of returning to spend the night dozing in the big chair by Harry's crib.

Now dawn was lightening the sky beyond her windows.

She stripped off the crumpled clothes she'd slept in, showered again, pulled on her tracksuit trousers and a clean shirt, and walked through the quiet corridors to the nursery.

Max was asleep in the chair beside Harry's crib, and the sight of the sleeping man caused so much chaos in Joey's still podgy belly, she crept away, needing to think.

Though how to think when she didn't know what Max was thinking?

She crept in again and checked on Harry, reading his notes to assure herself all was well. But there *were* no notes on Max, nothing to reassure her or give her a clue about the accidental father of her baby.

They had to talk.

He'd said he would be around for the operation, suggested taking things an hour, a day at a time—baby steps.

Could she, whose life was organised to the nth degree—apart from the nappies, of course—handle that?

'He's fine.' Her eyes had been on Harry, so she was startled to hear Max's voice. 'The nurse was here not long ago—I must have nodded off after she left.'

She looked down at the face of the man she didn't know and shook her head.

'I fell asleep,' she muttered, embarrassed now that he'd obviously sat there through the night.

'And a good thing too,' Max replied, standing up so he was very close to her. 'Now, while I think we both feel happier—more settled—when we're either here with him or close by, we also both know that we don't need to be here twenty-four hours a day, so unless this hospital is different from every other I've ever been in, there's an all-hours café somewhere close. Let's go and get some breakfast.'

Joey looked from the man, to the baby, and back to the man.

He was right. They didn't need to be there every moment of every day. Harry was being very well looked after without help from either of them.

And they *did* need to talk.

'Okay,' she said, and found herself smiling. Surely not because she was going to breakfast with this sleep-dishevelled man.

But walking out of the hospital with him, along the footpath in the early morning stillness of the street, her blood hummed in her veins, and her nerves thrummed with a pleasure she hadn't felt for a very long time.

'Let's have the special big breakfast,' he said, as they entered the café. 'Sausages, eggs, bacon, hash browns—anything else you'd fancy? Mushrooms? Tomato?'

He was reading from the huge board above the counter, and although Joey had fully intended telling him she couldn't eat that much for breakfast, she found herself agreeing, and even adding mushrooms to her order.

'And toast,' Max told the man behind the counter. 'Lots of toast.'

'I was silly, ordering that much, I'll never eat it all,' Joey told him as he guided her to a seat.

'Not to worry, I'll finish what you can't.'

He smiled—a smile that tilted up his lips and gleamed in his eyes—and Joey found her heart turning over in her chest.

Hormones, her head reminded her, and she nodded her agreement to the unspoken word.

'Talking to yourself?' Max teased, and she found herself smiling back.

'Always,' she said. 'Probably comes of being an only child. One of the nurses caught me at it last night.'

Stupid thing to say because right on cue Max asked what she'd been saying then, and she realised any explanation would have had to include her confusion over his entrance into her life.

'Who knows?' She shrugged off the question and began to play with the salt and pepper grinders on the table, moving them this way and that.

A large hand rested on hers, stopping their movement.

'We'll work it out,' he said, his voice deep with sincerity. 'Just because we can't see the way ahead right now, it doesn't mean it won't become clear in time.'

She lifted her head, saw the reassurance in his green eyes and felt her hands begin to tremble.

'I really do know that,' she said, moving her hands before he felt the movement. 'It's just that right now...'

She had no idea how to continue.

'You're tired, you're emotional, you're confused and most of all deep down you must be worried sick about the op that's ahead for little Harry. We doctors might pretend we can cope with anything, but when the patient's very close to us we feel all the doubts and insecurities and fears that non-medical people feel. In fact, we probably suffer more because we understand the procedures and processes and risks, and that's scary.'

Breakfast arrived before Joey had to reply. She nodded, and attacked the meal in front of her, diverted by the aroma of the massive breakfast and hunger she hadn't realised she was feeling.

Stupid thing to say—the stuff about things becoming clear in time, Max thought as he watched Joey lift her egg onto a piece of toast and break the yolk. How on earth would the way ahead become clear in a mess like this? And what was *he* doing, sticking around, getting more involved every minute he was in either Joey's or Harry's company?

Joey was right, Harry was *her* baby.

His involvement was accidental.

Getting all emotional on seeing her bump, then even more emotional actually being there for Harry's birth, didn't qualify him for fatherhood.

He'd be as bad as his father. He'd be always pulling against the traces that tied him to his family until finally he'd snap, as his father had done, and take off. Even as a young child he had known there was something wrong— something that made his father remote, angered by the smallest misdemeanours—different from other kids' fathers who kicked balls and joked with their sons.

'Aren't you eating?'

Joey's question brought him out of the past, but not before he'd been struck by a strong, inner and totally unexpected conviction that he could do better than his father.

'Just thinking,' he said, picking up his cutlery and attacking the now-cooling meal.

'Not very happy thoughts, if your face was anything to go by,' Joey said, and he shook his head—shaking off her comment and the gloom that delving into the past had momentarily cast upon him.

Tiredness, that's all it was.

'So, Africa next.' Joey looked up from the bacon she was dismembering, clear blue eyes studying his face. 'I'm pretty sure you said you'd been before, although not all of our conversations from the other night are crystal clear.'

He smiled at the way she made light of her labour.

'I've been there many times,' he told her. 'It's a big place, and there's always a crisis of some kind somewhere over there so medical services are in constant demand. This time, though, it's to a peaceful place, and I'm looking forward to being just a small part of something that could see the end of AIDS/HIV.'

'Preventative inoculation?' she asked, and he could see her struggling to remember more of what he'd told her as he'd held her hand and supported her during her labour.

'It's too soon for that yet, though it's well on its way. It's what I do. But my job isn't in a lab, perfecting vaccines. It's working on methods to get people to take vaccines when they're available. It's working with drug companies to make vaccines affordable. Even something like measles can still decimate populations. If you like, I'm the link between the boffins and the people. I go where I'm needed.'

'So, you're off when?'

Two days' time, originally, but he couldn't tell her that, or that he'd already changed the bookings for his flight.

'I'm not due to start work for a few weeks,' he told her, not mentioning the extensive travel plans he'd made to fill that time.

He was about to add, 'So I'm here for you until then,' when he remembered the things the sensible part of his brain had been telling him earlier. *Think before you speak, Max,* it told him now, right on cue.

He looked at the woman sitting opposite him. He'd hit her with the worst possible news and probably brought on her premature labour. Could he walk away, knowing she faced not only Harry's operation but the psychological adjustment to knowing it wasn't her dead husband's baby?

'I'm yours till then,' he heard himself saying, and knew it was the only decision he could have made.

For himself, as well as for her, apparently, as tension he hadn't known he'd been feeling eased from his body, and he returned to his breakfast with renewed enthusiasm.

Food. They both needed food.

And time—time always helped sort things out.

Was she pleased he'd made this commitment? She seemed more relaxed—talking about a visit the previous evening from her receptionist, Meryl.

He was thinking how lovely she was, a slight smile playing across her lips as she described Meryl's reaction to him being with her during her labour, when a mobile rang somewhere.

Joey's apparently, for she stopped talking immediately and began searching in her handbag.

'It might be the surgeon,' she muttered, and he could see her hands shaking slightly as she lifted out the mobile.

So it was natural for him to cover her free hand with his as she answered.

Wasn't it?

'He'll operate tomorrow morning, nine o'clock, and we can be there if we want.'

'Do you want?' Max asked, and Joey, who was still taking in the surgeon's words, looked at him blankly.

'Maybe I've got permanent pregnancy brain,' she said, knowing she must sound pathetic, 'but I can't seem to think.'

Max squeezed her fingers in his big, warm hand, and she wondered how long he'd been holding them.

'You don't need to think right now,' he told her very firmly. 'Just eat your breakfast and we'll decide later.'

'We?'

'Of course we. If you decide you'd like to be there, I'll be with you.'

Joey ate a piece of bacon while she considered this, then had to ask.

'Why? Why are you being so kind to me? To me, not Harry. The Harry part I can kind of understand, you probably feel it's the right thing to do, but me?'

Max smiled at her, and she wished she hadn't asked the question—hadn't done or said anything at all that might keep him anywhere in her vicinity because, postpartum hormones or not, she couldn't help feeling a strong attraction to this man.

'I have no idea,' he said honestly, spreading his hands and smiling even more broadly now. 'It's a question I keep asking myself. I imagine it's because you're part and parcel of Harry and the unexpectedness of what's happened, and on top of that you're not exactly hard to be kind to.'

He paused, then added, 'Now finish your breakfast and we'll go back to the hospital and decide what we want to do. Presumably, by "being there" the surgeon meant we could watch from afar—gowned and masked, of course, but out of the sterile area around the table.'

Joey shuddered.

'I'm not sure I want to be there. Being involved in neo-natal operations when I was training almost put me off paediatrics. Once I'd assisted in a few of those, I began to wonder if I shouldn't switch to some other specialty.'

Remembering, she smiled.

'Actually, it was Dr Prentice—the same surgeon who's doing Harry—who pointed out to me that I didn't need to get involved with newborns. He reminded me that neona-tology was only one branch of paediatrics.'

'What bothered you about it?'

The question was so unexpected—why would he care?— Joey paused before answering.

'I think it was the utter vulnerability of the babies. That

sounds silly because anyone under anaesthetic on an operating table is totally vulnerable, but somehow, when it's a tiny baby, it just seems worse. And then there's the size thing—the delicate balance of anaesthesia and all the surgery being microsurgery because they're just so darned small.'

Max was smiling again, and although it was a kind and understanding smile, Joey really wished he wouldn't. His smile—in fact, his presence—was causing her disturbances she didn't want to consider, let alone think about enough to understand.

'I'm happy to watch,' he said cheerfully. 'In fact, I'd like to—so if you feel Harry needs a parent somewhere nearby, then surely I would do.'

'While I wimp out?' Joey shook her head. 'No way!'

She concentrated on finishing her breakfast, partly so she wouldn't have to think about what lay ahead for Harry, but also so she didn't have to look at Max, leaning back in his chair across the table from her, watching her over the rim of his coffee cup.

Although eating while someone watched wasn't much fun, with the constant worry that a bit of egg might have escaped and be decorating her chin.

She set down her cutlery and pushed the plate away.

'I didn't leave much for you, but it's there if you want it.'

He set down his cup and smiled.

'Half a congealed sausage and a very cold bit of egg.'

He prodded the offerings with his fork then looked up and, of course, he had to go and smile again. Her bones melted completely.

What was wrong with her?

Hadn't she had plenty of men smiling at her over the years?

Hadn't she even considered some of them seriously, one seriously enough to think about marriage?

It wasn't as if she'd led a totally man-free existence since David had died!

So why was she going into bone meltdown over this man, especially when all he'd done had been to smile at her?

She stood up, knowing she had to get away from him for a while so she could sort herself out. She'd go back to the hospital and sit by Harry's crib and get her head together.

'Let's go back and sit by Harry's crib,' the man she had to get sorted in her head said, and she had to laugh.

'I'm sorry,' she said, when she finally pulled herself together. 'It's just that I'd had that exact thought myself at that exact moment.'

It wasn't quite true; her thought had been of her, singular, sitting by the crib, not both of them, but still…

Max didn't reply, still struck by the reaction he'd had to her carefree burst of laughter. How long since he'd heard a woman laugh out loud like that? Laugh at something as simple as a shared thought?

And since when did a woman's laughter send blood racing south in his body?

Lack of sleep—it had to be that.

He walked beside her back to the hospital, surreptitiously studying her. Not a small woman, well built, although a lot of that would be pregnancy weight.

Did it worry her, carrying extra weight?

Was she a weight-obsessive like two of his sisters, forever on diets and spending hours a week in the gym?

Considering the workload she must have, he doubted the gym part.

Harry was asleep when they reached the special care unit.

'I wonder why he'll have to spend fourteen days in hospital after the op?' she asked, startling Max out of his preoccupation with her lifestyle.

'Hey, you're the paed specialist,' he reminded her. 'Don't *you* know?'

'I don't do neonates, remember.'

She flashed him a grin.

'I do know it's to do with how soon he can take food through his mended intestine, but two weeks seems like overkill. And if my experience of expressing milk last evening was anything to go by, the sooner I can start feeding him myself the better.'

'We'll ask the surgeon—or Bob,' Max suggested. 'But in the meantime, could you tell me what you do know about duodenal atresia? Could there be complications?'

She was bending over the crib and turned to look at him, eyebrows raised.

'Stupid question—all operations carry a degree of risk,' he muttered.

'Not that stupid,' she said, smiling again and waving her hand towards the chair. 'You sit and I'll perch on the arm this time.'

He sat, a little warily because whichever way they shared the chair, proximity was inevitable and all his senses would be on Joey alert, feeling her warmth, smelling her woman's body, even hearing her breathe—though why that should be sexy, he couldn't imagine.

'I think,' she began as she perched beside him, apparently unconcerned by *his* proximity, 'that one of the biggest problems could be the ventilator. Remember Dr Prentice telling us he would be on it post-op?'

Max nodded, although he wasn't sure he did.

'Well, having to go onto a ventilator could make a newborn think he's back in the womb, as he doesn't need to do any breathing on his own, which means it can be a struggle to get him off it again. It's always a risk in newborns—the ventilator thing—and that's why, although he's having his oxygen supplemented in here, he isn't physically attached to a machine that breathes for him.'

Max reached out to stroke Harry's soft, soft skin.

'I think he'll manage coming off okay,' he said, his eyes on his son. 'He's a tough little guy.'

'And you'd know that, how?'

Max heard the tease in her voice and knew she'd be smiling.

'I just know,' he told her. 'Don't I, Harry?'

The baby moved, just slightly, in his sleep and they both laughed.

How long since she'd laughed with a man?

The thought wove through Joey's mind, along with one that seemed to think being able to laugh with someone was an important part of any relationship.

'The other concern the medical staff will have will be nutrition. They won't know how his stomach will react to breast milk—or anything else. I imagine he'll still be getting most of his nutrition through a drip. Then, at some stage, they'll begin to give him very small amounts of breast milk, probably through a nasogastric tube.'

'Which has its own complications,' Max put in. 'I *do* remember that part. If he's fed like that for too long, he'll object to having to work for his dinner and you could have trouble breastfeeding.'

He looked up at her.

'Were you intending…?'

Joey realised she was doing better when he was watching Harry and she was reciting nice safe medical facts, but when the man looked at her…

'Yes, because it's easiest, and there's always food on hand,' she replied, pretending she wasn't at all embarrassed discussing breastfeeding with a strange man.

Which she shouldn't be, of course, but inside she was squirming with discomfort over something so *normal*.

How could this be?

Was it more than the hormonal surge?

Was she sickening for something?

Lovesickness?

Not love, of course, but something similar, something juvenile—

'I've lost you,' Max said, leading her back from the messy track her thoughts had taken.

'Not really,' she said, but for the life of her she couldn't remember what they'd been discussing, her mind having been on the man, not the infant.

Somewhere outside church bells were ringing, sounding faintly in this little corner of the hospital.

'Pity he was born yesterday,' Max said. 'My mother used to say a little rhyme about children born on different days of the week. I know it starts Monday's child is fair of face and goes on from there. If I remember rightly, Saturday's child works hard for a living, while Sunday's child gets all the good stuff.'

'Sunday's child! It's Sunday!' Joey muttered in absolute panic.

'Hey, what's wrong with that?'

Max had obviously heard the panic for he turned to look up at her, taking one of her hands in both of his in a comforting way.

'David's parents—they phone me on Sundays. Every Sunday, without fail, unless they're overseas, which they are at the moment, but, oh, Max, they're coming here on their way back to Melbourne. How am I going to tell them? When should I tell them? *What* am I going to tell them?'

She was asking *him*?

He was still having difficulty coming to terms with the situation himself, and Joey was asking *him* for help?

Max tried to think, but the situation was so far beyond belief there was no logical way to think it through.

'Do you have to tell them?' He asked the question cautiously, gently, not wanting to upset her more than she was already upset.

'Of course I have to tell them.' She hissed the words at him, not yelling because of Harry but definitely upset.

Nonetheless, he had had his reasons for asking, so he might as well keep going.

'Why?'

Her eyes widened in disbelief.

'Because it's the truth,' she muttered. 'I can't have them thinking Harry's David's baby if he isn't!'

'Why not?' Max persisted, but this time he thought he should help her out by at least offering some reasons for not telling. 'They have phoned you every week, Joey, even before you decided to have the baby, so it follows they look on you as family. The baby is yours, won't they love him for that reason alone?'

He could tell by the scowl on her face that he wasn't getting anywhere.

'And who will it hurt for them to believe it's David's? I imagine they've been really looking forward to having something of their son given back to them.'

Anguished now, the blue eyes!

'But he *isn't* David's, he's yours!'

Max stood up and eased her into the chair as tears began to leak from her eyes, slow and fat and apparently unnoticed, so he took out his handkerchief and wiped them away, Joey being lost in a world of misery that was closed to him.

She took the handkerchief from him, mopped her face, then leaned back in the chair and reached out to rest her fingertips on Harry's arm.

'I can't *not* tell them,' she eventually said, calmer now—determined.

'Truth at all costs!' Max muttered to himself, and as memories surged in his head he wanted nothing more than to walk out—to walk away from Joey and Harry and the mess that one stupid, avoidable accident had caused.

Not that he could...

Joey saw the shadows of emotion passing across Max's face and remembered something he'd said at some stage of their short acquaintance—something that had made her think some confession of truth had hurt him badly in the past.

'Please sit down again,' she said, and moved, intending to let him have the chair.

'No, stay there,' he said, resting his hand on his shoulder to urge her to stay. A strong, warm, ever so comforting hand.

And something as minor as a hand resting on her shoulder distracted her so when he did sit she had to think back to what she wanted to say—or ask!

CHAPTER EIGHT

'YOU SAID SOMETHING before about truth hurting people,' she finally managed. 'Was it back at the office, or since then? Not that it matters, but did the truth hurt you sometime?'

She looked up into his face, still shadowed by an emotion that looked very much like sadness.

'Apart from when a couple of fiancées told me what they thought of me?' he said flippantly.

But the flippancy was a cover, she knew that from the way he studied her, and once again she wondered if he'd answer the question—truthfully—or avoid it. His smile, slight though it was, gave her the answer.

'Not me, but the eldest of my sisters. She was pregnant with her first baby, Mum's first grandchild, and on the way to hospital to deliver it, her husband decided he should confess all—and told her about an affair he'd been having while she was pregnant.'

'Great timing!'

Max nodded.

'She was okay at first—she was already having contractions and didn't have time to think about it—but after the baby was born, she—'

'The marriage broke up?' Joey guessed.

'Almost immediately,' Max replied, 'and she became depressed, seriously depressed. She might have been a candidate for postnatal depression anyway, and the shock exacerbated it, but she was in and out of hospitals for years—still is. Mum and my sisters between them have brought up her daughter, Maya.'

Joey tried to imagine how she would have felt but it was so far outside her experience it was impossible—apart from hoping fervently that *she* wasn't going to suffer post-natal depression.

She looked at Max, who was still lost in his memories.

'She's special to you, that particular sister?' Joey guessed, and he nodded.

'Very special,' he said, smiling slightly now. 'She was like a second mother to me, and during my teenage years I could tell her all the things—ask all the questions—I couldn't tell or ask Mum. Our father left us when I was five—the youngest of the tribe—and I think Phoebe took his place in a lot of ways, giving Mum far more support than he ever had, and looking after all her younger siblings, especially me.'

Joey could feel his hurt, and understand it…although…

'Should he not have told her, the husband? Would continuing to deceive her been better?'

Max sighed.

'Hell, Joey, I don't know. It's just that I can't help thinking of those people, David's parents, looking forward to their grandchild and then learning it's not their grandchild at all. Wouldn't it be like a death to them? Won't they grieve for that baby? Feel the loss?'

Joey frowned up at him, obviously not liking what he'd said. So shut up now, his inner voice suggested, but did he listen?

'How would it hurt them to not know?' he continued, and the frown on Joey's forehead deepened.

He felt a quixotic urge to smooth it away, to run his fingers over that creamy skin, to tell her everything would work out in the end.

Not that he was in any position to offer advice about

happy endings. He was more confused than he'd ever been in his life.

He didn't like the thought that had just occurred to him, but he had to put it forward.

'Are you worried they might guess if you don't tell them and they see me around Harry too much? Do they visit as well as phone? I'm away a lot anyway and...'

He stalled, torn between emotion and common sense, but it had to be said.

'Would it be easier to not tell them if I opted right out of the picture?'

It hurt more than he'd expected to actually say the words—like a slicing knife wound, in fact—but...

'Are you listening to what you're saying?'

Even muttered, the words were so filled with disbelief they seemed like physical objects flung into the air around them.

'You're talking about deceit. Not a little deception but an ongoing one—a forever-and-ever deception. You think that's okay? And as for you opting out, as you put it—you're not really in, are you? Oh, you've been great and I appreciate all you've done, but you'll be off again before long, you said so yourself. You're really nothing more than a sperm donor, only not anonymous. So is it better for Harry to have a father who bobs up now and then, or not have one at all? That's what *I* need to consider.'

Gobsmacked didn't cover what Max felt.

'Nothing more than a sperm donor?' Max managed to mutter, but Joey was already halfway out of the unit, and from the stern look on the face of the nurse who was just entering, it would be better if he didn't follow.

The woman fiddled around the crib, every crisp movement telling Max she'd heard some part of the conversation and was definitely on Joey's side.

As she stalked away, she confirmed his guess, turning

to say, 'You shouldn't be upsetting her!' in a very reproving voice.

'Of course I shouldn't,' Max told Harry.

But Joey was right, wasn't she?

He *would* be off again in less than a month, even sooner if he was called up to join an emergency response unit, travelling to an outbreak somewhere in the world.

And *that* work had become his life—as Joey's work was hers. Not that he didn't enjoy the ordinary work he did—lecturing, research. But it was the ERU work that gave him a buzz and an enormous amount of satisfaction.

Could he give it up?

Would he *have* to give it up if he wanted to play a major role in Harry's life?

And if he gave it up, would he be replaying his father's role—there but chafing against the bonds of family life? Eventually giving in to the urge to bolt?

He reached into the crib and ran his finger lightly down Harry's arm, then studied the sleeping infant, while a mixture of pride and fear and uncertainty and, yes, he thought perhaps love, churned inside him.

Maybe the question was, could he *not* be involved in this child's life?

Back in her room, Joey sat on the bed, staring at the breakfast of cereal and cold toast that had been left on her table.

Cereal and toast! Exactly what she'd ordered because cereal and toast was what she always had for breakfast.

Boring, boring, boring cereal and toast!

Have I become so dull that a breakfast that included sausages and bacon and mushrooms has unsettled me? she demanded of herself.

Not dull exactly, she objected, but maybe a tad regimented.

And regimented when one had a demanding job was good, wasn't it?

Of course it was, so why was she sighing?

She hated to admit it, but the problem wasn't really the excitement of bacon and mushrooms, much as she'd enjoyed them—the problem was she'd enjoyed the breakfast so much because of the company.

Because of Max Winthrop.

Here today and gone tomorrow Max Winthrop…

Maybe gone even now. Hadn't he just offered to opt right out of the situation?

Not that her *child* could be called a situation…

And had he made the offer solely because of the looming phone call from David's parents and the 'tell or not tell' argument, or had he already been looking for a way out of a very sticky situation?

Some innate kindness in the man had caused him to stick around once her water had broken, and then, apparently, being there for the birth—actually holding Harry as he was born—had made him feel a bond with the child he'd accidentally fathered.

Was that enough for him to commit to a child for life? Or, once the initial curiosity wore off, would he vanish from Harry's life?

And how would *that* affect Harry?

This time Joey groaned, timing it badly.

'What's wrong? Are you in pain? Where does it hurt?'

Max settled beside her on the bed and put his arm around her shoulders. He tucked her hair behind her ear and peered into her face.

'Tell me!'

An order!

But could she?

Was if fair to share her doubts with him?

He'd been so good—sticking with her through the birth and then promising to stay on for Harry's op—wouldn't sharing her doubts about his fathering ability be unkind?

'Nothing's wrong,' she muttered. 'I was just thinking.'

'Painful thoughts?' he prompted, but she shook off his

oh-so-comforting arm and stood up, dragging her hair back into a scrunchy, although she knew how unattractive that must make her look right now.

Did it matter?

She realised it did, which led to the next realisation—that while his coming and going from their lives might not bother Harry, it would bother her.

Stop this relationship—whatever it is—right now! her head ordered.

But the operation? her heart whimpered.

'I think I'll go back and sit with Harry,' she said, but her escape was thwarted when a tap on the door announced the arrival of visitors—Lissa, her friend from childhood, accompanied by the eldest of her children, Joey's goddaughter, Grace.

'We've come to see the baby,' Grace announced, wrapping her arms around Joey's waist and looking up into her face. 'Mum says I can't hold him, but I can look, can't I?'

'You certainly can,' Joey told her, dropping a kiss on the girl's forehead, trying desperately to sound rational and together, although she knew Lissa must be studying Max, now standing by the bed, and storing up a million questions.

'Sorry! Lissa, this is Max Winthrop. Max, Lissa and Grace Jones. So, Grace, you're in luck. I was just going off to sit with Harry. You coming, Lissa?'

If she says no I'll have to kill her, Joey decided, because there was no way she was leaving her insatiably curious friend with Max—not for an instant.

Max must have caught the vibe for he led the procession out of the room, saying, very casually, 'I'll see you later, Joey.'

'And just who is that mesmeric man?' Lissa demanded as they went their separate ways down the corridor.

Mesmeric?

Was that how Lissa saw him?

Had he mesmerised Joey?

'Well'?' Lissa demanded.

And Joey stalled—her mind switching off the mesmeric question but then going blank. There were so many ifs and buts rattling through it, no words could possibly come out.

Not sensible words, anyway.

Until something Max had said—who knew when?—came back to her.

'He went to uni with Harry's paediatrician,' she said, then, knowing that wouldn't stall Lissa for long, continued, 'Did you know I'd called him Harry? And did Meryl tell you about the problem he has—duodenal atresia, a blockage in his duodenum—so he needs an operation? It's tomorrow, and although I know it's a simple op and quite common and the surgeon's fantastic, I can't help feeling sick about it.'

Which was both the truth and enough of an admission to divert her kind and empathetic friend completely.

'Oh, Joey,' Lissa said, putting her arm around Joey's shoulders where Max's arm had been. 'Poor you! But you know he'll be all right—although I don't suppose all the assurances in the world make a jot of difference when it's your baby.'

And so she rattled on, soothing, comforting, the stranger in Joey's room forgotten.

For the moment, at least.

Joey led the visitors into the unit and introduced them to Harry.

'He's getting supplemental oxygen and they're monitoring his lungs and heart and blood oxygen levels, and they have to feed him through drips and drain his little stomach. Hence the wires and tubes all around him.'

'Oh, Joey,' Grace breathed. 'He's beautiful! Can I touch him?'

'Very gently,' her mother said, before turning to Joey and repeating the compliment.

'He *is* beautiful. He hasn't got that crumpled, scrunched-up new-baby look at all.'

Joey studied her son, seeing him through her visitors' eyes, seeing, for the first time, the beauty they were seeing. Dark eyelashes rested on pearly-pink cheeks, his little nose had shape and character, while his lips were pinker than his cheeks, beautifully shaped like—oh, nonsense, as if she could see similarities in lips!

But the image of Max's lips remained in her head until Lissa drew her attention to the shape of Harry's head.

'You can see he'll have brains—a beautifully shaped head,' she was saying, while Grace squealed with delight as Harry clutched at the little finger she'd sneaked into his hand.

'He's holding me, he likes me,' she said, and to her further delight, Harry opened his eyes to see just what was disturbing his sleep.

Huge blue eyes moved to take in his surroundings, and Grace's excitement could barely be contained.

'So what's involved with this operation?' Lissa asked quietly, and Joey explained, taking her time, aware visiting hours would be over soon, which lessened the chances of her friends running into Max.

Lissa had just moved on to questions about Joey's labour when the chimes went.

'Just as soon not think about that now,' Joey told her, ushering them out and accompanying them to the front entrance. 'I'll tell you all about it some other time, preferably without small children present.'

Lissa accepted that with a smile and a kiss on Joey's cheek.

'As long as you're through it and okay,' she said. 'You are okay?'

'More or less,' Joey answered, skirting the truth but knowing Lissa would assume the 'less' part was just concern over Harry's op.

Which it, partly, mostly, was.

So, she thought when she'd seen her visitors out and was walking slowly back to the elevators to take her up to her room. *For all your anger at Max suggesting deceit, you haven't exactly come out with the truth yourself.*

But surely this was different.

'You want a coffee and something to eat? Sandwiches, salad, something light for lunch? Not coffee or tea. I had a vague memory of the coffee ban reaching past the birth so checked it out.'

Max had appeared from nowhere and was guiding her towards the café in the foyer of the building.

'Were you lurking here to catch me and tell me things about coffee?'

He smiled and her mind went blank again.

'Not really,' he said. 'I mean, yes, I was lurking to catch you, but so we could have lunch together, not to tell you things you probably already know about coffee. Do you drink coffee anyway? Normally, I mean?'

He shook his head and smiled again.

'I don't know anything about you.'

The statement was so plaintive Joey smiled back at him.

'Not much to know about me but, yes, I do drink coffee—gallons of it when I'm working—so it's been total deprivation.

'Which has to continue for the next few months,' Max said, obviously pleased with himself for finding out whatever he'd found out. 'Apparently only about one percent of the caffeine we consume goes into the blood, so once the baby is about three months old a few cups of coffee a day won't hurt. But newborns find it harder to process caffeine—it takes far longer to get out of their bodies. So while you're expressing milk for the milk bank and while Harry's little, you'll have to continue to suffer.'

It was a stupid conversation, but he was looking so

pleased with himself she had to pretend she didn't know about the caffeine and thank him for telling her.

'So, I'd better stick with chai a few months more,' she said, then felt a tremor run through her as he put an arm around her waist to guide her into the café.

This was impossible—silly conversations and the slightest of touches, and she was going gaga.

'I've had Masala chai all over India but here people seem to drink it differently. Do I ask for something special?' Max asked, pulling out a chair at a corner table and somehow getting her to sit on it.

'Chai latte they usually call it because they add milk and serve it in a glass like a coffee latte. But no food—my lunch is probably waiting in my room right now.'

'So, one chai latte,' he said, and she looked up and caught the slightest of smiles on his face. A barely-there smile, yet it made her heart skip a beat and her stomach lurch.

He's just being kind to you, she reminded her misbehaving internal organs. If there's one thing you know about Max Winthrop, it's that he's a kind man.

Kind to everyone, most likely—children, dogs, old ladies, street people...

She studied his back as he waited in line at the counter, shifted upwards to have a good look at his head—well, shaped like Harry's.

A kind, intelligent man.

But a restless man, an adventurous man who put himself in harm's way.

'So, what did she think?' he asked, when he returned to the table with her chai latte and what looked like a short black espresso for himself.

'Who think about what?' Joey asked, stirring half a teaspoon of sugar into her drink before looking up at him.

Max stared at her in disbelief. Did she really not know what he was getting at?

'Who, your friend, and the what, of course, is about Harry. What did she think?'

Joey smiled at him.

'She thought he was beautiful.'

'And that's all?' Max was having a hard time keeping his voice at a suitable level for private conversation in a café. 'What about me? What about Harry not being David's baby?'

The pink lips that invariably attracted his attention in Joey's face—they'd felt so soft, tasted so sweet!—made a round O of surprise.

'We didn't talk about that,' she finally said, her voice small rather than muted.

'You mean you didn't tell her?'

'Well, no.'

She sounded as puzzled as she looked. He took a very deep breath and then another before he spoke again.

'So I've been pacing the foyer for the past hour, wondering what's happening, wondering how this first test is going of telling one of your friends the truth—the truth you believe is important—and you didn't tell her?'

'It wasn't the right time.' Joey spoke defensively, but her flushed cheeks gave away her embarrassment.

'And me? Did you not have to explain my presence in your room?'

The colour in her cheeks deepened, but puzzlement had given way to anger in her eyes.

'What was I supposed to tell her? Yes, I thought I would be able to explain about you fathering Harry, but you've been so good to me—so kind—sticking with me through my labour, being there for me when I heard about Harry's problem, promising to be there for the op. So I couldn't bear for her to think badly of you, and if I told her you'd be opting out of fatherhood, which you'd just said you *could* do, then she *would* think badly of you.'

She faltered to a halt then added, in a *very* small voice, 'Or I thought she might, and I wouldn't like that.'

Her anger had faded and she was so obviously stressed Max couldn't help but cover her small hand, where it rested on the table, with his much larger one.

He ran her slightly muddled reply through his head and came to the bit that had bothered him.

'You're worried about people thinking badly of me?'

She looked up at him.

'No—well, yes. Kind of.'

She moved her hand to clutch at her head. 'Honestly, my brain's just gone haywire! I do hope it's something to do with the hormones and that it will eventually get back on track.'

He had to smile.

'I don't suppose it could be due to the shocks you've had the last few days. It's not exactly been a normal, peaceful weekend.'

'No, that's just an excuse,' she muttered, 'although you're not helping. Oh, I didn't mean that—of course you're helping. But not knowing what's ahead for us, for Harry, that's not helping.'

He was about to tell her he understood when she spoke again, looking directly at his face—into his eyes.

'And I know you're in just as bad a place right now. I mean, you've had just as much of a shock as I have, and I can understand your not knowing which way you want to go as far as Harry's future is concerned, so I'm not blaming you for all my muddled thinking, but it isn't making it easier.'

He shook his head. Torturous as it was, he could understand her decision, but for how long could she hold out not telling her friends, and all so they wouldn't think badly of him?

They are not people you *know,* the nagging common

sense voice in his head reminded him, *so it doesn't matter what they think of you.*

But what if he stayed involved and they did become friends?

He swallowed a swear word.

'It's impossible,' he said aloud. 'So let's go back to what we'd decided when—yesterday? Take it a bit at a time. Get through today and the operation tomorrow, and hope a way ahead might become clearer with time.'

'Hmph! That's lovely positive-thinking stuff, but where does it get us?' she grumbled.

'Have you got a better idea?' he retorted, his own mind so tied in knots it was hard to hide his exasperation.

To his surprise, Joey smiled.

'Well, I did turn off my mobile to avoid a call from David's parents if they happened to be somewhere they could phone from, and perhaps we could get the staff to post a "No Visitors" sign on my door.'

He had to smile back, although the first part of her answer bothered him.

'Won't they worry if they can't get you, David's parents?'

'I've emailed,' Joey replied, and he saw the colour rise in her cheeks again so he wasn't surprised when she added, 'I told them Harry had come early and had a little problem that an operation would fix and I'd be in touch once he was safely through it.'

Ha! A victory to him in the 'tell or not tell' debate, but Max felt no pleasure. The colour in Joey's cheeks told him how embarrassed she must feel at not telling them the whole truth.

Not to mention turning off her mobile.

'You're not gloating,' she pointed out.

'Of course I'm not. I'm not totally insensitive and I realise just how hard it's going to be for you to tell them.'

He didn't add, *if* you tell them, mainly because he'd been

thinking more about it and discovered just how tricky a situation it could be.

Joey picked up her now cool drink and sipped at it. Of course he wasn't insensitive—in fact, apart from David, he was probably the most sensitive man she'd ever met.

Or was she confusing kindness with sensitivity? Had the matter-of-fact way he'd passed her her underwear back when she'd been getting dressed for the hospital been nothing more than kindness?

She didn't think so.

'It's like a maze, isn't it?' she said.

And to her surprise, he not only smiled, but said, 'That's definitely a great metaphor for what's going on in *my* mind. I think I've got it sorted and go down one path and something comes up that proves a dead end, so I go another way and, wham, same thing. I wonder if there are problems humans have to face that logical thinking just can't sort out?'

'But if we don't use logic, what can we use?'

He looked at her and smiled again.

'Emotion? Isn't there such a thing as emotional thinking?'

'Not in my headspace,' she told him, although some part of her brain was willing her to agree. 'I gave up on emotion as a guiding force in my life years ago.'

'But now you've got Harry,' Max protested.

'And I'll love him with my head—intelligent love. That *has* to be possible!'

She watched Max's face, almost daring him to argue with her, but all he said was, 'Do you think so?'

Well, she had up until yesterday, but she was pretty sure the wavering in her convictions was hormonal, not sensible.

'Of course,' she said, stalwartly denying the questioning bit of her brain.

'So what's the difference?'

Lord, the man was stubborn! But how to explain without admitting just how many bits of her heart she'd lost to love when first David and then her entire family had been taken from her?

'There's no obvious difference,' she said. 'How could there be? Harry will know I love him—he'll always know that.'

'But he'll be loved from your head and not your heart?'

Damn the man for homing in on that. He *was* sensitive.

'So?' she demanded, giving up on the chai and setting the glass down too hard so it sloshed onto the table. Grabbing napkins to mop it up enabled her to avoid looking at Max, so she wouldn't see what was probably disapproval on his face.

Max was pretty sure the confused, distracted woman opposite him—the one fussing with damp napkins and making things worse—wasn't anything like the normal Joey McMillan. Not that he wasn't confused and distracted himself.

The confusion, given how recently he'd heard the news of his fatherhood and the dramas that had followed, was normal, but the distraction had blue eyes, and soft lips, and blushed like a sixteen-year-old on a first date. Or did girls have their first date much earlier these days?

Was he *ever* glad Harry wasn't a girl!

See, confusion!

But to get back to the distraction, it was the physical attraction he was feeling towards the mother of his child that was the big problem. He was reasonably sure it was totally one-sided, and it felt almost indecent to be feeling the way he did about her when she'd had a huge shock, a slightly preemie baby, and one with a problem at that.

No woman could be more vulnerable than Joey was right now, so there was no way he could take advantage of that vulnerability and do anything about the attraction. In fact, he had to avoid revealing any evidence of it.

Yet if ever a woman needed a comforting hug, a touch

of a hand on her shoulder, or a quick cheer-up kind of kiss, it was Joey.

'I'll get you another drink,' he said, and moved away from the table without waiting for her reply.

The really bothersome thing with all this was that he had no idea *how* to work out a plan for the future.

For *his* future as far as Harry was concerned, especially given the fact that a relationship of any kind with Harry would naturally include some kind of relationship with Joey.

For someone who'd always relied on logical thinking to map his path ahead, this was a whole new world because if there was one thing he *had* realised, it was that logical thinking didn't work when emotion was involved.

When his heart was involved?

Was this what Joey had been talking about, loving with the head and not the heart?

Well, he could understand, given the terrible losses she'd suffered, why she hoped she might be able to manage that, but he was pretty sure he couldn't.

He carried the fresh chai latte back to the table, which had been cleared of debris.

Cleared of the woman causing his confusion as well.

He looked around, aware he was frowning, although more worried than annoyed.

'She said to tell you she was going back to her room,' a passing waitress said, then she grinned and added, 'I hope you drink chai.'

Max dumped the coffee on the table and left the café.

She'd left the message—did it mean she wanted him to follow her?

Or that she'd had enough of him for the day?

He stood in the foyer and muttered some choice swear words in his head, directed at himself, not at Joey.

How could a man used to making split-second decisions

in some of the most dire emergency situations be unable to decide whether to go to her room or not?

She was a woman, and he was good with women. Or, these days at least, he was good at decision-making about them—able to choose which ones with whom he could have a mutually enjoyable relationship with no animosity or angst when it ended or he departed to a distant part of the world. He liked women, as friends as well as lovers, and had always thought they quite liked him.

But *this* woman!

He didn't have a clue.

Except that he wanted her.

It was highly inappropriate.

Yet he was already heading for the elevator, and it was only when he reached the maternity floor that he forced himself to go and sit with Harry, rather than further confuse his mind and body by heading for Joey's room.

CHAPTER NINE

SHE MUST HAVE changed her mind about the room, because she was sitting in the big chair, Harry in her arms, leads and wires and tubes carefully arranged around her. He stood in the entrance for a moment, looking at her, thinking that even with the paraphernalia of the hospital, it was still a beautiful mother and child cameo.

Until he saw the tear plop down onto Harry's belly.

'What is it? What's wrong?'

He stepped towards her and squatted beside the chair, realising as he looked up into her face that it hadn't been the first tear to fall.

And all his good resolutions to stop touching her vanished at those faint stains on her pale cheeks. He put his hand on her arm, stroking it gently, feeling her warm skin, her softness.

'I never cry!' she muttered at him, and he had to smile because he believed her. Anyone who'd gone through childbirth so stoically would be adept at keeping tears in check.

'So why now?' he asked gently. 'Is there something else wrong? Has Bob been in? Or the surgeon? Have they delayed the operation?'

She shook her head, and sniffed—something else he was reasonably sure she never did.

'So tell me,' he persisted. 'It must be something.'

Joey looked into the craggy face of the man she really

didn't know, hesitated for a moment, then blurted out what, to her, given her earlier conversations with him, had been a shocking discovery.

'I love him,' she said, tightening her hands on the very small 'him' in question.

Max smiled at her.

'I'm pretty sure that's included in the job description of being a mother,' he said gently. 'And didn't we cover this earlier?'

He eased himself upright and settled on the arm of the chair, sliding a very comforting arm around her shoulders.

Comforting her, that's all, she reminded herself.

'So why the tears?' he persisted.

'It's not with my head,' she all but wailed. She really *was* losing it! She definitely never wailed.

'It's with my heart,' she admitted grimly. 'Just like that—I looked down at him and felt it in my heart. I didn't want that, Max. Definitely didn't want it because that kind of love is just too painful, too all-consuming—too much to bear when things go wrong.'

She could feel tears welling again and willed them away.

'It wasn't that I didn't intend to love him, or expect to, but like I said earlier, I really thought I could do it with my head. I see children who've been adopted and I talk to their parents who often worry about bonding—worry that because the child isn't genetically their child, the bonding thing might go wrong.'

She sighed and thought she'd better stop this maudlin nonsense, but Max's 'Might?' told her she'd better finish what she'd started.

'I'd remind them of the majority of animals whose young are usually up-and-about within minutes of their birth, seeking out their first feed. But human babies are totally dependent on whatever adult happens to be around to care for them, and it's their total dependence on their carer that builds the bond. That was *my* theory, anyway.'

'I like it,' Max said, smiling at her. 'And I'm sure adoptive parents are very grateful to hear it. In fact, one of my sisters would have been very happy to hear it after her first baby. She thought there was something wrong with her that she didn't immediately feel overwhelming love for the demanding little human that had come into her life. In fact, she confided to me that she thought the instant bonding stuff was all a myth, so maybe you're right.'

'In theory,' Joey grumbled.

'Everyone's different,' Max reminded her. 'Anyway, is it so bad to love him with your heart?'

Even as he said the words he remembered the losses she'd already suffered—her husband and then her entire family. Remembered her talking about loved ones being hostages to fate.

And he understood her fear.

He tightened his arm around her shoulders and drew her close so her head rested against his hip.

'I'm sorry, stupid question,' he said, 'Although, from the little I know of you, I doubt you'd ever have been able to separate your head and your heart as far as this little fellow is concerned.'

He felt her head move as if she might be nodding in agreement, but then she just sat, still and silent, her head resting against him—giving him enormous pleasure, although she couldn't know that.

Was she lost in the past? Reliving those losses—the ones that had damaged her heart?

His arm tightened around her shoulders and he leaned forward and dropped a kiss on her shiny dark hair.

She didn't move away, although she did look up at him, eyes wide, lips parted...

Asking to be kissed?

Probably not, but it was as natural as night following day for him to lean a little lower and kiss those parted lips.

Gently, softly. Asking nothing. Promising nothing. A quick, light, 'I'll be here for you' kiss.

Except it didn't end there.

Had she responded, or had he imagined that?

Whatever, the result was the same.

The kiss deepened, exploring first, still tentative but learning through touch and taste, teasing...

Deepened again, demanding now, desire morphing into need as he suckled on her lip, slipped his tongue into the moist, warm invitation of her mouth, met the urgency he could feel building in her response with a passion that he hadn't felt before—didn't understand.

His heart was hammering against his ribcage, his lungs desperate for air, but how could he not keep kissing her?

A whisper of sound escaped her—a whimper? a moan?—and he caught it, swallowed it, wanted more, hungry for more. His hand was moving on her arm, sliding up her neck, his fingers burying themselves in fall of her thick, dark hair, tangling there, holding her, wanting more of her so desperately he thought he could hear a moan escaping his lips as well.

He'd reached the summit of some of the world's highest mountains, he'd revived a baby that had been buried underground for days after an avalanche near a village he'd been working in, he'd had a hundred experiences that had given him indescribable excitement and pleasure, yet nothing came even close to what he was feeling—to the thrill he was feeling kissing Joey.

'Oh, please, not in front of the children!'

The voice broke them apart, flushed and panting—well, he was definitely panting and she was flushed, delightfully flushed, stirringly flushed.

Max looked up at Bob, who was standing beside the big chair, smirking down at them, a nurse hovering behind him.

'Getting to know each other?'

Max conquered the urge to punch his old mate in his smiling face, settling on a growled 'You'll keep,' instead.

'I've just come to check Harry out, and run some preliminary tests before the op tomorrow. The surgeon says you'll both be there. Me too. I assist for Prentice whenever I get the chance.'

He checked the chart at the end of the crib then bent over to look at Harry, gently palpating his stomach.

'I'll take some blood—just to check he's not harbouring an infection—then move him into another room for scans. You two are welcome to wait here until he gets back—that's if you don't want to get a room.'

Max scowled at him. Bob, obviously, had never grown up, and was gloating over his adolescent humour.

Joey, who'd sprung away from Max's embrace as soon as she'd heard Bob's voice, was already on her feet.

'I'll see you later,' she said to Max, walking carefully around him as if he'd suddenly become contagious. The nurse who'd accompanied Bob had already wheeled the crib out of the unit, Bob following, which left Max sitting in the big chair wondering just what the hell he should do next.

Follow Joey?

Wait for Bob to return and tell him if the scans had been okay?

Would Bob return with Harry, or would the nurse wheel him back?

And the big one—would Joey want him following her?

Big mistake, kissing him back like that.

Seeking refuge in her room, Joey slumped down on the bed, something that was becoming too much of a habit. Max was obviously a man who scattered kisses around like confetti. He kissed the way some people touched—connecting with whatever female who happened to be near him.

And comforting though a couple of those kisses had been, she certainly shouldn't be taking them seriously, and most definitely should *not* be mistaking them for anything more than confetti.

Bad enough that Harry, young as he was, had sneaked under her guard and into her heart, but opening it up to more pain by letting Max in would be a disaster.

Yes, he was a kind man, caring and empathetic, but she didn't need a man of any kind.

And Harry?

That part of it was a simple enough equation. No father or a now-and-then father—which would be best for Harry?

Her own father had always been around—detached from time to time when he'd been busy—but always there for her.

Had being an only child made her closer to her parents?

Oh, Lordy, Harry was an only child. That brought up a whole new set of problems. Why, when she'd decided to have him, had she not considered that?

Her mind took flight and suddenly she was thinking about family, as in mother, father and children.

Brothers or sisters for Harry. And the father image in this fantasy was most definitely Max.

Except he wouldn't be there—not all the time.

Would that stop him being a good father?

Hadn't there always been wanderers in the world? Sailors who were away for months on end, astronauts living in the space station circling the earth right now, and, more prosaically, the men who worked the big mines and gas wells right here in Australia, away three weeks, home for two.

Families could adapt.

Couldn't they?

She sighed and immediately regretted it as a light tap heralded the arrival of the source of her confusion.

'I'm sorry for embarrassing you like that in front of Bob and the nurse,' he said, as he came and sat beside her on the bed—stirring up all the overactive nerves she'd been trying to calm down.

'Embarrassment's the least of my worries.'

She must have sounded a little tart for he stiffened and would have moved off the bed if she hadn't rested her hand lightly on his leg.

Not a good idea as he immediately placed his hand on top of it, and although a memory of a kids' game, hand on hand on hand, flitted through her mind, it was lost in the more recent memory of the kiss—of her reaction to the kiss—of her reaction to something as simple as his hand on hers on his warm, solid thigh.

'Could all that's happened, and our bond through Harry, be overstimulating us?'

Max realised he probably shouldn't have blurted out that question, but it had followed him from the special care unit to this room—accompanied him, really, nagging away in his head.

Joey turned towards him and smiled.

'Now, that would be a really, really satisfactory explanation, wouldn't it?'

She appeared to consider it for a moment then added, with a smile teasing at her lips, 'You think?'

Max ran his free hand through his hair, probably making it more unruly than it usually was.

'I've no idea what to think—can't think at all, in fact—beyond how soon I can kiss you again, and whether we could lock the door.'

'Probably not, it's a hospital,' Joey replied, but he thought he detected a hint of gloom in her voice.

Because they couldn't lock the door?

He could shut the door...

And he did, returning to his position on the bed, wrapping an arm around Joey's shoulder, lifting her chin with one finger so he could study those blue eyes and that creamy skin, the still reddened lips—

'Game to try it again to see if it answers anything?'

Her eyes told him she was wavering—worrying—but

when he brushed his lips across her mouth he heard that little sound again. Not a moan or whimper, more a plea.

But not for him to stop, apparently, for when he hesitated she came to life, moving closer, straightening so her lips met his this time, testing, tasting, her tongue probing his teeth, his mouth, her arms around him now, hands moving on his back, his shoulders, kneading his muscle and sinew, sliding down to grasp his waist, then up, between them, on his chest, brushing lightly over his nipples.

There was hunger in the kiss, and in the touching, in the little noises that escaped. But not, he thought, a seven-year hunger—not a need for a man and any man would do. No, something in the kiss told him it was personal, and for whatever reason—the shock she'd had, the excitement of giving birth, the burden of Harry's problem—the attraction she was feeling was for him.

And you know that because? muttered the cynic who was never far away.

Because I feel it too, for her.

There, it was out, at least in his head. One thing sorted.

So he gave himself over to the kiss, wholly and solely, giving and taking in the increasingly frenzied embrace they were sharing.

They parted slightly, mainly to replenish air supplies, but Max wanted to look at her, to really see her—flushed, panting slightly, desire still sparking in her eyes.

She studied him in turn, detaching one hand from his shoulder for long enough to push back a lock of his hair that had fallen into his eyes.

Her fingers stayed on his face, straying there, tracing out the lines, smoothing at an eyebrow, trailing down his nose to touch his lips, outlining them so softly he shuddered at his touch.

Which made her smile—a mischievous smile that caused a riot in his senses and a further hardening of the bit of him he'd hoped to keep quiescent.

'Not that I'm agreeing to it or anything, but does a convenient marriage include sex?'

This time the interruption came in the form of a loud tap on the door followed by the arrival of a brusque, officious nurse.

'You're late for your physio and you've missed your time on the breast pump machine,' she said, not bothering to hide her annoyance.

Max stiffened, upset by the woman's tone—ready to do battle.

But Joey quietened him with a warning touch on his hand.

'I used the breast pump earlier, and I didn't know about the physio,' she told the intruder, her voice soft and apparently apologetic enough for the other woman to unbend slightly.

'There should be a card. Probably on your lunch tray. And you haven't eaten your lunch either!'

The disapproval was back in the last sentence, but Joey was already on her feet, searching for a card, finding and reading it, smiling apologetically.

'Well, I'd better go. I'll at least have time to learn a few exercises to help me get rid of my tummy.'

She was out the door in a flash, leaving Max sitting on the bed, feeling like a first-year med student—totally out of his depth.

'Afternoon visiting hours don't start until three,' the dragon informed him. 'Fathers-only between visiting hours.'

'I am the father,' Max told her.

And earned a 'Hmph!' as the woman sailed through the door.

But her reaction didn't bother him one bit. He was far too busy trying to work out why actually saying the words had caused such a rush of emotion in his body, and even more confusion in his head.

Even more than the kiss?

Joey's question and the word 'marriage' had been cavorting in there, but they'd been silenced, packed away. But *I am the father*—they were just words, but they had so much power they'd knocked all other thoughts completely out of his head.

Just what *did* it mean, being a father?

Could *he* be one?

Or should be back out right now?

He walked back to where the source of all the questions lay, not sleeping at the moment but looking around at the world he'd come into—a limited view of it, admittedly. He was looking at him, although Max knew he probably wasn't registering faces yet.

A nurse was there, the one who spent most time with Harry.

'Can I hold him?' he asked, and she nodded for him to sit in the chair, then lifted Harry out and arranged the tubes and wires so they didn't tangle.

'Unbutton your shirt so he's on your skin,' she told Max, who found his fingers shaking as he obeyed.

Then she settled the little infant against his chest and as Max cupped his hands, one below the buttocks and the other on his back, he felt his son snuggle into him, and the little head turn, mouth open, seeking milk most likely, but to Max it felt just like a kiss.

'I'm your father,' he said quietly, aware of the commitment he was making—unable to do anything else.

He savoured the words as he gently supported the little form against his chest.

'Your dad,' he added quietly and felt his heart open like a flower, spreading its petals to embrace the sun.

'Forever and ever, kid!'

CHAPTER TEN

JOEY TRIED TO follow what the physio was telling her. The exercises had assumed mammoth importance in her head, but the rash question she'd asked Max earlier—the one about convenient marriages including sex—was rattling around in her brain, bumping into her good intentions about exercise.

'You're not quite with me,' the young woman told her. 'But if you do the exercises properly and keep them up for a few months, you'll be really glad you did.'

'I know,' Joey groaned, going back to the beginning of the sequence. 'It's just—it's just that Harry, my baby, has this op coming up in the morning. I know he'll be okay, but…'

It wasn't quite the truth—well, not about the op but the excuse for her distraction.

'Well, in that case, you should try even harder with the exercises,' her smiling torturer told her. 'Exercise is the best antidote to worry.'

She was right, and Joey tried harder, concentrating on what were really very simple exercises, working up a sweat in the end. And when her mind strayed, it was to Max himself. To images of him—not the silly marriage business—and the images pushed her just that little bit further, made her work that much harder.

She went back to her room, hoping she could have a

quick shower before Max materialised in his usual fashion. This plan was thwarted by finding two friends sitting
on her bed.

'Lissa phoned us,' one offered excitedly.

'We peered into the special care unit on our way, but
there were only three babies in there and all of them had a
parent,' the other said.

'One of whom was a particularly attractive man who
was holding his baby like it was the most precious thing
on earth.'

Her friends were talking over each other, but a parent
by each crib?

Max? Joey wondered. Holding Harry?

'Harry's due to have an op in the morning—they were
doing tests and things on him when I was there, so they
might have taken him off somewhere,' she said, busying
herself with the flowers they'd brought and unwrapping
little gifts.

Diverting them and herself with her appreciation of the
gifts.

'Oh, you've no idea how much I needed some hand
cream—I packed in such a hurry I didn't think of things
like that.'

She opened the tube, offered it around, then began
smoothing cream into her hands.

'And I brought body lotion that's great for stretch marks,'
her other friend chimed in. 'When Lissa told us about your
contractions starting we guessed you'd have packed in a
hurry. Now tell us all about it.'

How could she?

What to tell?

How much?

The uncertainty of her situation hit home once again.

'Let's go down to the café in the foyer,' she suggested,
aware the cause of that uncertainty could come wander-
ing into her room at any moment. Her shower would have

to wait. 'They have great chai latte and as I'm still off coffee, it's what I need.'

Her friends were only too happy to accompany her, but the question of the future was looming large in Joey's head. She couldn't keep avoiding the truth about Harry's parentage, but telling people opened up such a tangle of ifs and buts and maybes that right now she couldn't begin to explain.

'Hey, that's the gorgeous man,' one of her friends remarked as they caught a glimpse of Max coming along the corridor.

Joey ushered them into the elevator, but this time her mind had picked up on her friend's description.

Gorgeous?

And Lissa's word had been mesmeric!

Joey threw up an image of Harry's father in her head—all too easy to do these days—and studied it. She'd registered attractive, liking his tall, loose-limbed figure, but then he'd just become Max.

Did it matter that other women saw him the way her friends obviously did?

It shouldn't—

'Hey, dreamy, we have to get off here unless you want to go back up.'

The café was doing its version of a high tea, so they drank their tea and ate delicate little sandwiches and tiny morsels of cake, Joey keeping the conversation on the food and Harry's problem and the operation—anything other than talk of her labour and the man who'd helped her through it.

They sat on until the chimes sounded and she could walk her friends to the front door and out into the fresh air beyond. Guilt over what she was keeping from them wormed its way inside her. Although she knew when she *did* tell them, they would understand just how confused she was right now and empathise with the reasons for her silence.

As long as she didn't put off the telling for too long. But how long was too long?

Until she had some idea of what the future held—Max or no Max—it was hard to talk about the situation.

She stood in the doorway, looking out at the busy street beyond the boundaries of the hospital grounds. Had it only been two evenings ago they'd pulled up here? Only forty-eight hours since she'd met the man who'd turned her life upside down in more ways than one?

And the big question—the L one!

Was it possible to fall in love in such a short time? Or was all that she was feeling towards Max nothing more than a mix of attraction, gratitude, postpartum hormones and total confusion?

She sighed and made her way back to the maternity floor, detouring towards Harry's crib—he was asleep and there was no sign of Max— but there were two other babies and their parents in the unit. They'd had it to themselves up until now.

So it *had* been Max her friends had seen—Max *holding* Harry.

Oh, dear!

Had holding his son had the same effect on him as it had on her?

Had that little scrap of humanity dug his tiny fingers into Max's heart as he'd done to hers, grabbing hold of it forever?

She headed into the bathroom, hoping a long hot shower might wash away some of the confusion churning in her body and mind.

And in her heart?

Well, she admitted to herself, she wasn't going to wash away Harry's grip on it in a hurry, and maybe Max wasn't quite there yet.

He was waiting for her when she emerged, fortunately

dressed because she'd wandered half-clad out of the shower to find a nurse or a housekeeper in the room before now.

He'd obviously been back to wherever he was staying, for he was in neatly pressed, tan chinos and a darker tan polo shirt that, for some obscure reason, made his eyes look greener.

He *was* gorgeous, *and* mesmeric!

But the hitch in Joey's breathing and the hammering in her chest told her this wasn't an entirely objective assessment.

Her hair was damp and hung in twining tendrils around her face, and her eyes held the startled look that was beginning to make his heart still momentarily.

Convenience, Max reminded himself, and very nearly spoke right then.

But he held back, aware this woman was special—aware she deserved more.

'Come out to dinner?'

She looked even more startled, then grinned at him.

'I'll have the nurses in this place calling in anorexia specialists because I'm not eating any of my meals.'

He smiled back at her because smiling at Joey was so easy.

'They're nurses,' he reminded her. 'They know how bad a lot of hospital food is.'

He paused, waiting for her to speak, but she'd picked up a tube and was rubbing hand lotion on her hands.

'So dinner?'

'I guess,' she said, looking up at him—not smiling now.

'Well, don't rush me with enthusiasm,' he said, and she did smile then, although her voice was subdued when she spoke.

'It's *such* a muddle, isn't it?'

'Only if we make it one,' he said firmly, sure he had the answer, and anxious now to put it to her. 'Are you up to a short walk? I've booked a table at a restaurant by the river, but we have to walk through the park to get there.'

'A walk will do me good,' she said, more positive now, though hardly brimming with enthusiasm.

He waited while she fussed around, finding her phone and a little handbag—women stuff that always amused him.

Had she caught his thoughts that she said, rather tartly, 'It's easier for men, they have a multitude of pockets for these things.'

But the fussing, even her slight reprimand, warmed him in some undefined way.

Little indicators of family?

Confirmation that the path he'd chosen and hoped to lead her onto this very night was the right one?

Uncertainty clutched suddenly, biting into him, but he'd thought this through, it was the way to go…

'Well, are we going?'

Her tone was still tart. Was this a good start? Should he kiss her first? Now? He wouldn't be able to in the restaurant, so perhaps—

She was already out the door.

Was his presence always this disturbing? Joey wondered as she all but marched towards the elevators.

Or was she finding it so because of the personal thoughts about him that had been running rampant through her head?

There were people in the elevator, so many she was forced to stand very close to the man causing her such problems. Not that she minded close, but here in the elevator it suggested a kind of intimacy, as if a little bubble of space enclosed just the two of them—the two of them made one.

Awkward? Not at all—and that was part of the problem. This physical acceptance of their togetherness when, really, did it exist?

Could it exist so soon?

Once out, they were apart again, until he took her elbow as they crossed one busy street and then another, taking her hand to lead her down into the park, under the arbour of bougainvillea, off that towards the river.

Holding hands was a different kind of intimacy.

'Are you listening?'

She stopped and turned towards him. She couldn't lie.

'Sorry, have you been talking? I was miles away.'

'I gathered that.'

He wasn't exactly grumpy but definitely put out.

'I'm listening now,' she told him. 'So start again.'

'Now she's giving orders!' he muttered, but she thought she caught a smile in the words.

'I was telling you about my job but I've realised it's too complicated to go into as we walk so I'll wait until we're sitting down.'

She frowned, thinking back.

'The tropical medicine stuff? Are you working on something new? A breakthrough of some kind that it's so complicated?'

'Other work,' he said, obviously determined not to elaborate until they were seated.

'The vaccination stuff?'

'Will you stop guessing? We're nearly there.'

Was he getting huffy?

He sounded huffy, but the fact that the question arose in her mind was further evidence of just how little she knew of this man.

Although picking up on moods of one's companions took time, so why should she be able to guess at his feelings?

'I think I'll be glad to sit down and listen to you tell me whatever it is,' she told him. 'My head's so jumbled with conflicting chatter I can't think straight.'

He smiled down at her—he couldn't have been too huffy—then dropped a kiss lightly on her lips.

Which felt wonderful but didn't help the jumbling chatter.

They were seated in the restaurant, drinks ordered—French champagne.

'I checked on the internet. You can drink it, and it goes out of your breast milk at the same time it goes out of your bloodstream, so one unit in two to three hours.'

Joey had to smile.

'You're a very nice man,' she told him. 'And as I'm not going to be expressing more milk until morning I can probably have two glasses, although I should warn you, after nine months of abstinence I could get tipsy.'

'I somehow doubt that very much,' Max said, taking her hand across the table and holding it, even though the waiter arrived at that moment to pour their drinks.

'Shall we order then talk, or talk first?'

Joey lifted her glass.

'First things first,' she said. 'Cheers!'

'And here's to Harry,' Max responded, touching his glass to hers.

But she could see the need to say whatever he wanted to say was hovering in his head, obvious in the shadows in his eyes. She was about to suggest they talk before they ordered, but the waiter was already there, hovering, so Joey scanned her menu, suddenly excited about a dinner that wasn't something she'd cooked herself, or a takeaway—her usual treat for herself.

'I'll have the rack of lamb with the pomegranate jus, roasted beetroot and baby potatoes.'

'*Bleah*, fruit with meat!' came the response from her fellow diner. He looked up at the waiter. 'I'll have the T-bone. I've been told it's something special.'

The waiter agreed and departed, leaving the two of them, one waiting to talk, the other waiting to listen. A serious talk, apparently. Joey wondered if Max was feeling the same tension that was coiling through her.

Not that he seemed perturbed until he lifted his glass to her again and took a fair gulp of his drink.

'I want to tell you about my job,' he said, and this time she didn't interrupt with guesses. 'I told you about the rescue on Everest.'

She nodded and watched his face, seeing shadows but determination as well. *A man with hidden depths,* she thought, then he was talking again.

'It made me think about emergency situations, gave me an interest in them, and the more I read about different disasters and considered how the world could respond to them, the more I felt connected—as if the rescue on the mountain had given me a definite direction in my life.'

He paused, and she was aware he was waiting, not for a response but to assure himself she was with him so far.

She nodded, sipped her drink, interested because it wasn't something she'd thought much about herself.

Too personal?

Too close?

Possibly.

'Go on,' she said. 'I *am* interested.'

'Over the years, the world in general, and some countries in particular, have developed excellent modes of quick response. Air transport, developments in all kinds of fields has meant that specialist units could be set up to be deployed at what's virtually a moment's notice to any part of the world.'

'I've heard of them,' Joey admitted. 'They come fully self-contained, don't they, so the helpers who go in can house and keep themselves for a month.'

'Close! Every unit is different, but basically they are self-contained—shelter, food, power, water and sanitation equipment is standard. They're called emergency response units, and under that banner are a lot of different units, including, in the medical field, basic health care, referral hospital and a rapid deployment hospital.'

'Very necessary things, I would think.' Joey was drawn into the story, but wondering just where Max fitted in.

He answered immediately.

'So's telecommunications and a base camp, and water and sanitation, but we'll stick with medical. Australia doesn't have complete units, but we do offer medical personnel to the units that other countries have on standby. My normal work is research into contagious diseases, but that means I can be free in emergencies. I'm on call to the Canadian Red Cross, which has what is called a rapid deployment hospital. It's a small unit that can be wherever it's needed within forty-eight hours of any disaster. We're set up to be on site for ten days, and by that time can let the organisation know whether the bigger hospital is required or just a basic health care ERU.'

'Anywhere in the world in forty-eight hours?' Joey asked, and Max smiled at her.

'Well, we've never had to go to Antarctica but I imagine we could get even there in that time.'

'I am amazed, and awed, and slightly ashamed that I didn't even know such things existed. So, you're there ten days, then what?'

'We come home, or, if necessary, because we're small and mobile and don't have a lot of equipment, we can be used as a mobile clinic in another part of the country if required.'

'You don't cross over and join the staff on the bigger hospital?'

Max shook his head.

'I do go back to my normal research. Deployments are rarely more than ten to fourteen days, although in earthquake situations you can't always get out when you want to—aftershocks can close airports or roads that were previously open. So if you stay on you lend a hand.'

She was sure he did, but the words 'earthquake' and 'aftershocks' had rattled her, a smidgin of fear sneaking into the soup of emotions the man had already caused inside her.

'So I'm not always around,' he said, just as the waiter returned with their meals. 'On the other hand, it's not as if I'm off for a couple of weeks every month. I might go a year without a call-up.'

Was this conversation leading somewhere? Joey wondered, but the delicious aroma of her meal distracted her, and they ate and chatted, she asking questions about places he'd been, he answering, sometimes warily so she imagined there'd been a lot of horror in some of the situations he'd gone into so nobly.

He'd scoff at the word, she knew that much. The way he spoke this was just a job he loved doing, probably because he knew he was good at it. But as the meal ended she could feel tension building in the air.

Had he been told to be on standby?

It seemed ages since she'd seen or heard the news—was there a catastrophe going on somewhere in the world?

'Are you about to tell me you won't be here for Harry's op? It's okay if you're not. I'll be fine.'

She hoped she sounded braver than she felt. She'd grown accustomed to having Max around.

His answer was a smile and a squeeze of her fingers. Somehow, after their dinner plates had been removed, he'd regained possession of her hand.

'There's no standby warning or time for fancy dinners when a call comes in,' he told her. 'No, I wanted you to know—to understand what I do and why I have such doubts about being able to be a good father to Harry.'

Joey felt her heart melt.

'I doubt he could have a better father,' she said, and felt his fingers tighten once again on hers.

'That's good,' he said, 'because I want to ask you something. You don't have to answer right away, but I'm going soon to Africa—it's the last trip I'll be doing as part of the research I'm working on. I'd like to know—to be sure— I'm not doing this very well...'

He let go of her hand, poured them both more wine, then fished around in his pockets, patting first then delving, producing a very small, rather battered little box.

'One day I'd hope to get you something more than this, but for now I wondered... It was my grandmother's, she left it to me and I've carried it with me ever since for luck. But now, the marriage of convenience thing—giving Harry two parents...making a family—would you...?'

Max wasn't sure how he'd got that far in the proposal, because his tongue was thick and kept cleaving to the top of his mouth, and his mind had gone blank so he had to search through it for every word, and now Joey was sitting there like someone who'd been turned to stone.

He'd made a mess of things. It was a huge mistake. Why on earth would this woman want to tie herself to him?

Any woman really?

He just wasn't marriage material.

'What are you thinking?' she demanded.

He frowned, puzzled that his question had been answered by a question—or had he not asked a question?

'Right now,' Joey persisted, 'and don't bother telling me you're not thinking anything because I can practically read all the terrible thoughts running through your head.'

'Fair enough,' he said, and even managed to smile at her. 'I was thinking I'd made a mess of things. Thinking how this is so different from the other times I proposed. I was playing at romance. But this somehow seems solid. Good. But why would any woman in her right mind want to tie herself to a bloke like me? I'm also thinking how badly I might have embarrassed you just by asking—forcing you to answer me when you're probably feeling so sorry for the poor fool you'd find it hard to say no.'

Her answering smile held something—a little spark of mischief? He wasn't sure but it gave him hope.

'And if I don't say no?'

Hope and disbelief warred within him, joining a sudden spurt of anxiety as well—suppose he hurt this woman as he'd hurt others?

'You'd say yes?' He blurted out the words. 'But you barely know me!'

'Backing out?' she teased, a whole lot more mischief in her smile.

'Well, no!' The denial was so weak he knew he had to get a grip. 'Definitely not, but I don't want you to feel pressured.'

He stopped, took a deep breath and blew it out—loudly.

'I'm making a total hash of this, aren't I?'

She chuckled.

'You are,' she said, but kindly. 'And considering the practice you've had, you should be doing better.'

'I just thought maybe if we settled on not marriage right away but some kind of arrangement, the future might look clearer. I know you must be torturing yourself about what to tell your friends and David's family, and I thought, if we had some kind of commitment, it might give you backup. You wouldn't have to worry about what your friends might think about me if I didn't commit to Harry because…'

He paused, reaching the crux of things—a place he probably should have been earlier.

'I *am* committed to Harry,' he said. 'You weren't to know but I held him earlier. He's mine and I'll be a father to him however and whenever I can. I'm committed, Joey, now and forever!'

CHAPTER ELEVEN

IT WAS AN unmistakable declaration of intent, and Joey couldn't help but believe he meant it.

Would it help her tell people, knowing the baby's father was right behind her all the way, willing to stick around and be a father? Willing to *marry* her, for all it might be a convenient marriage?

Did he take her silence for assent as he passed her the little, battered box?

She took it from his trembling fingers, opened it and smiled. Inside was a delicate ring, white gold, she suspected, with a square old-fashioned setting—a dark blue sapphire nesting in a border of tiny diamonds.

'It's beautiful,' she breathed.

'Put it on,' he said, his voice as breathless as hers had been.

She lifted it out, about to slide it on. For some reason she'd stopped wearing David's ring years ago. She no longer felt married. But now she hesitated. Putting a ring back on this finger felt like such a big deal.

'Are we doing this just for Harry?' she asked.

His face grew grave.

'I *think* it's for all three of us.'

'You do know we barely know each other,' she reminded him.

'We've plenty of time to remedy that,' he said, still grave

but his mood lighter somehow, as if he, too, felt an underlying whisper of physical desire that had somehow sneaked into the words.

'You do it,' she said, passing him the ring, aware in every cell of her body that she was, right now, foolishly or not, committing herself to this man.

He took her hand and slid the ring onto her ring finger, smiling that it fitted so well.

'It was meant for you,' he said, and she knew in that instant it hadn't been offered to either of his earlier fiancées.

Somehow they paid the bill and left the restaurant, not exactly running but moving with swift strides to the first dark patch of shadow they could find.

Her need to wrap her arms around this man, to hold and be held, was obviously echoed in him, for that's all they did at first. They just held each other close, making a silent, physical commitment to each other, strengthening their togetherness.

And shadows being abundant, they walked, and stopped, and kissed, and held, and kissed again, every embrace strengthening the ties between them, every kiss reaffirming the commitment they had made to each other.

Joey felt a peace she'd never known before settling in her heart, while the chatter in her head stilled completely.

Back at the hospital it seemed natural to go straight to the special care unit, Max introducing her to the two new arrivals, two baby girls, one father and one mother. Joey settled on the chair beside Harry's crib, Max in his usual position on the arm of it.

Joey leaned her head against his thigh and tried to think, but now it was happiness rather than worry and muddle blocking her thought processes.

So don't think, she told herself. Just feel, and be content with that, because no matter what anyone might think, it *was* possible to fall in love in just forty-eight hours!

Not that she'd mention *that* little snippet of information

to Max. She was pretty sure love didn't feature in the re-
quirements for a convenient marriage.

But much as she'd tried to harden her heart—to protect it from future pain—first Harry and now Max had
sneaked right in.

'You go to bed so you're not too tired in the morning.
I'll sit with him.'

Max's fingers were trailing through her hair as he spoke,
the feel of them so pleasant it took her a while to grasp
his words.

'But if you sit all night you'll be tired too.'

He smiled down at her.

'I won't sit all night. As long as he knows we're around
most of the time, he'll be okay.'

Max shifted from the arm of the chair, taking Joey's
hand to help her up.

'I'll walk you to your room,' he said, because there was
no way, on this momentous night, that he was leaving her
without a good-night kiss.

The cheeky smile she gave him, before saying
good-night to the other parents, told him she'd guessed
his agenda. But it also told him she wasn't averse to it.

It held promise, this convenient marriage...

Back by Harry's crib—much later—he tried to work
out how he felt.

Settled?

It seemed such a mundane word for the multitude of
emotions he'd experienced that day—the last couple of
days, in fact—but that's how he did feel.

Settled!

He reached out to rest his fingers lightly on Harry's leg.
Yes, he was settled with a son and now a woman who would
be his wife. They'd make a family, the three of them together, and the idea was suddenly immeasurably exciting.

By midnight he knew he needed sleep, so headed back
to his apartment. He really should move closer, although

Joey was likely to lose her bed at the hospital any day now. Maybe he would stay at her place. Was that presuming too much?

They *were* engaged, after all…

His body stirred, but other commitments loomed. He couldn't not go to Africa—and that was only a few weeks away…

Joey woke slowly, coming out of the deepest sleep she'd had since she'd arrived at the hospital.

Pleasure flooded through her as she felt the ring on her finger, followed by anxiety as she thought of Harry's op.

Uncertain when they'd want to take him through to theatre, she dressed hurriedly and went through to the unit. No Max, but a nurse who told her it would be three-quarters of an hour before they moved him.

'Have you had breakfast?' the nurse asked, and when Joey shook her head, the nurse shooed her away.

'Go and eat,' she said. 'It's important you keep up your strength, especially as you're going into theatre for the op.'

Joey kissed her son lightly on the cheek, then obeyed the nurse. It *was* important that she ate, even if it was only the boring cereal and toast she'd ordered, and which had been delivered, for her breakfast.

But at the toast stage she began not to worry but to feel a little niggle of concern. Max was usually around by this time of the morning.

The woman who came to take her tray was bursting with news—almost indecently cheerful as she regaled Joey with details of a horrific accident less than a kilometre from the hospital. Apparently a train had derailed, hitting the support of an overpass, which had collapsed on the train, injuring and trapping passengers.

At least Max wouldn't be on a train, was Joey's first thought, even before she felt a wave of sympathy for the victims. Many of the injured would be coming to this hospital. From what the woman had said, it was definitely the closest.

She remembered all the disaster planning sessions and disaster drills she'd attended and knew medical staff would be called in from all over the city.

Could she help?

And not be there for Harry's op?

She knew she couldn't—she'd be too distracted to do any good, and emergency medicine was a whole different field.

It was time to go with Harry into theatre and still no Max.

Not that she didn't know exactly where he was! Her certainty was so great it was far more than a guess.

Could you know someone so well after so few days?

What she did know of him was that he'd somehow got involved in the train wreck—just walking past, most probably—and, adrenaline junkie that he was, he'd been drawn in.

That was unfair—the adrenaline junkie bit. After all it was what he was trained to do, what he was an expert at. Wasn't it?

He'd heard the noise, the screeching protests of metal tearing, the roaring of an engine unable to continue on its way, the thunder of falling bricks and masonry, and already—although possibly only in his mind—the cries of those in shock and pain.

He ran, not charging in panic but with loping strides, towards the noise, aware of the irony of the situation—aware that he was letting down the woman who'd agreed to marry him within hours of his proposal.

Both the woman *and* his son. The latter disappointment hurt him most, although Harry would be blissfully unaware of his absence.

Yet still he ran, reaching the scene within minutes, assessing the situation, checking first with a shocked railway official that power had been turned off, looking for any signs of fire—a telltale wisp of smoke, a flicker of light where there should be none.

He could hear the jangling medley of emergency vehicles' sirens and knew they'd soon be on the scene, but he was here now and trained for this.

'Stay away from the part that's under the collapsed road,' he told the men and women already scrambling down onto the tracks to assist in any way they could. 'Help the passengers in all the other compartments get out. Bring them over here, away from the train.'

He wasn't surprised when these willing volunteers all went off to do as they were told. In situations like this, people liked to be organised—needed to be told how they could help.

'The firies will bring equipment to shore up the bridge above the wrecked carriages,' he said to the still hovering official. 'But I'll try to get in there now, to see just how badly people might be injured. I'm a doctor—I've done this kind of thing.'

The man patted his shoulder with a trembling hand and took over directing helpers to the undamaged carriages from which shaken passengers were now being helped.

Max entered the first carriage, skewed to one side and tilting dangerously but still fairly intact. It must have been the second one that had jumped the rails and hit the support.

Easing past the people being helped out of it, he entered the second one, bending down as the caved-in part of the roof made access difficult.

Those who could move were struggling out, some helping others, some just intent on escaping the horror that had struck the early-morning commuters.

The cries and moans of pain were clearer here, while helpers shouted frantically for more help, to reach a friend, a wife, a child…

Max eased forward, reaching one such helper who was clinging to the hand of someone trapped beneath a tangled mess of metal and upholstery.

'It's Mandy. She's always on my train,' the young man said, and Max slid his hand down the youthful-looking arm, feeling for the girl—shoulder, neck, pulse.

Strong and steady.

Relieved, he reached further in, feeling for the wetness of blood. Nothing he could reach.

'Stay with her, talk to her,' he told the young man. 'Someone will bring equipment soon to cut her free.'

Max felt his way down what had been an aisle, feeling for the injured in the gloom. Someone caught his hand.

'Help me, please!'

He spoke quietly to the unseen person, again following an arm up to a shoulder and a neck. Thready pulse...

'Are you bleeding?'

'Not much, but I can't breathe.'

Max felt around, found the carriage seat that had impacted on this victim, tried to lift it, even just slightly, to ease the pressure on the person's chest—his lungs—although aware if there was an open chest wound, he could be making things worse.

The fingers holding his tightened, whispered thanks, a faint voice assuring him he or she—the voice so soft he couldn't tell—would be okay until more help came.

'Find someone else,' the voice said, so Max moved on. And on!

The noise of generators told him the experts had arrived, so the bridge would be jacked up, temporarily secured above the damaged carriages and full rescue teams and paramedics would be flooding into the carriages.

But the man he'd found beneath a seat, clutching at his damaged leg, might not last that long as blood was pumping sluggishly from a wound in his upper leg.

Femoral artery damage?

The flow sluggish because his blood flow was compromised somewhere else?

Or was his heart struggling for some other reason?

It didn't matter, Max knew. He padded his handkerchief and pressed it to the wound, wriggled round until he could pull the laces from one of the sneakers he'd put on so he could jog up to the hospital.

Thanking the heavens for the fashion of long laces, he tied the lace around the man's leg, holding the handkerchief in place, praying someone would be there to release the man before the lack of circulation to his lower limb affected the tissues there.

'Anybody in here who can move, please try to make your way towards me.'

The voice held enough authority for Max to obey, wriggling himself back along the narrow tunnel even before the man added, 'We're about to lift the bridge, and the train will probably move and we don't want any more injuries.'

'I'm a doctor, I can help,' he told the man when he finally reached him.

'Good! Go talk to the triage people—you'll recognise them once you get outside.'

Joey followed Harry's crib into the theatre, her fingers twisting the ring Harry had put on her finger only last night.

She had no doubt he was just up the road, and understood that it was where he had to be, but would it always be like this?

He'd warned her about his lifestyle—that he could be called away at any moment—but what if it was always when she needed him?

Was she selfish to be thinking this way?

It wasn't as if Harry was in danger. He had the best surgeon in the state, the op was a simple one, and two and a half days ago she hadn't even known Max.

So why was her stomach churning? It wasn't with anger exactly, and not really disappointment…

She took the gown and mask a nurse handed her, said thank you, put both on, then stood where she was told so she could watch her old mentor operate on her very new son.

Max's son!

Was this why his last two fiancées had given up on him? Because of the churning when he wasn't there?

Was she so weak?

So pathetic?

Surely she was made of stronger stuff.

She felt for the ring on her finger, but this time, as she twisted it, she remembered what he'd said.

I've carried it with me always—for luck!

He didn't have his ring for luck!

He was in danger and the ring was right here on her finger!

And *she* was feeling sorry for herself?

Worry over Max's safety now joined her concern for Harry and it took every bit of inner strength that she possessed to focus on her child—tiny and vulnerable on the operating table—and the operation.

Harry would be on the table now. A clock chiming somewhere nearby reminded Max where he should have been. He kept patching up the passenger who'd been allotted to him, but in his head he pictured Joey, there alone in theatre, seeing a knife cut into their child.

Melodrama, Max? the cynic muttered in his head, and Max knew it was right. Harry was in the very best of hands.

And Joey?

He wished with all his heart she hadn't experienced what life with him could offer quite so soon.

She was a doctor, she'd understand.

Wouldn't she?

'Is it worse than you thought?'

His patient's voice saved him from further mental torture, recalling him to the task his hands were undertaking automatically.

'Why?' he asked, startled out of his meandering thoughts.

'You look so worried.'

He smiled at the elderly man and finished bandaging the gash on his arm.

'You'll be fine,' he assured him. 'We could send you to a hospital to have this cleaned better and maybe stitched, but the emergency rooms will all be very busy and you'd probably have to wait for hours. Do you have a GP you could see some time today?'

The man agreed his own doctor would fit him in.

'Once I tell him I was in the crash he'll be only too pleased,' he added. 'Everyone will want to know about it.'

Max smiled and wished him luck and moved on to the next patient.

They took Harry to the neonatal intensive care unit after the op, and Joey was sitting there beside his covered crib when Max came in. One look confirmed where he'd been. He'd obviously showered as his hair was still damp. He was wearing clean clothes under a theatre coat, but there were scratches on his face and his arms.

He limped towards her and panic filled her chest.

'You're hurt!'

He looked surprised.

'Me, no, but I had to come straight here to say I was sorry, and just look at Harry. He's okay? There was this crash, you see, and I was almost there.'

'I heard, I guessed it's where you were,' Joey said crossly, worry still fluttering in her chest, 'but why are you limping if you're not hurt?'

He looked down at his feet, covered with the soft cloth they used for theatre protection. He then lifted one of them.

'No laces in this sneaker—it keeps coming off, even under the theatre cover. Bob loaned me clean clothes—he has an apartment here—but his shoes are two sizes too small. And his pants are too big—this belt is barely holding them up. But I didn't want to waste time getting here.'

She was so relieved she wanted to hit him, but he was already asking about the operation, about how Harry was doing.

Joey kissed his scratched cheek.

'Harry's fine,' she assured him. 'Go and rest. You look exhausted.'

He took her hand, looked into her face.

'I am. And you? I hate that this had to happen, but it's what I do.'

'And you could no more ignore it than you could stop breathing,' Joey said, kissing him again, this time on the lips.

She didn't add that she wasn't sure how she felt about it. Didn't share her doubts about her ability to cope with what was obviously a very important part of his life.

Did he read those doubts in her eyes that he squeezed her hand, touched her shoulder, and said quietly, 'We'll talk about it later.'

Then he was gone, a tall, rangy, man, limping along to keep his shoe on...

CHAPTER TWELVE

To JOEY'S AND probably Max's delight, Harry recovered quickly, off the ventilator within twenty-four hours and out of the NICU within forty-eight.

Somehow Max had established a schedule, whereby he stayed by Harry's crib at night, with Joey doing the day shifts. It had begun when he'd reminded her that she needed rest to ensure her milk supply—hardly a romantic notion but a thoughtful one nonetheless.

But Joey was disappointed because it meant they saw less of one another, and she was beginning to believe that a marriage of convenience, for Harry's benefit, was all Max wanted.

A marriage of convenience with sex, she amended, remembering the heated kisses they'd shared on the occasions when they'd been alone in her room—or one day in the park, in daylight, when he'd insisted she take a walk in the sunshine.

'I'll be back to sit with him tonight,' Max assured her, four days after the operation—the day Harry was due to start feeding on her breast, having tolerated the breast milk she'd been expressing for him. 'And I'll be here in the morning when they try him on the breast.'

Harry, always Harry. Max was so clinical and detached, the medical staff the 'they' who would 'try him on the breast'.

And Joey snapped.

'Hey, it's me who'll be helping him breastfeed for the first time, not some unrelated "they."'

Max looked surprised.

'You're upset?'

'Now why on earth would you think that?' she retorted, before her anger faded out with the swiftness of air from a pricked balloon.

Because she knew his next question would be why, and how could she explain, when she really didn't know herself?

Had it been the stark realisation that their relationship *was* just a convenient one that had thrown her so much?

He'd certainly be puzzled if she told him that, because it was obvious that's all he was considering it to be.

But he didn't ask why, simply took her in his arms and held her close, and, weak female that she was deep down inside, she leaned on him and made the most of his warmth and comfort.

She went to bed—so Harry's breast milk supply would be top-notch, of course—but something had shifted between them.

Since the op, or since the handing over of the ring?

She wasn't sure and really didn't want to worry about it for fear her worry would communicate itself to Harry, and the first natural feeding would prove difficult.

Not for Harry, as it turned out!

With Max and a senior nurse watching, he fussed a little in the beginning then took to this new supply of food with great enthusiasm, so much so there was talk of him going home much earlier than they'd expected and excitement began to build in Joey.

But in bed that night the excitement turned to apprehension.

Would they *all* be going home?

All *three* of them?

To *her* home?

If things between her and Max had become awkward here where they could get away from each other, how much worse would it be in her apartment?

And would Max be expecting to be invited to live in her apartment or would the idea horrify him?

Why, oh, why had she not thought through all this stuff? At least talked to him about it?

Worrying over it wasn't doing her any good. Max would be in with Harry, giving him the night feeds with milk she'd expressed earlier. She'd go and talk to him right now.

And say what?

She turned over in bed, pulled the pillow over her head and tried to sleep.

'How about you come up to the coast with me today?' he suggested two days later. 'Get right away from the hospital for the day? Harry will be fine without us, you've got enough expressed breast milk there to feed a dozen babies, and you could do with a break. I need to see the dean at the university but shouldn't be more than an hour with him. You can take the hire car down to the beach and walk in the sand, splash in the waves, think about when we can take Harry to the beach.'

She pushed away, stupid disappointment flooding the weak female part of her because yet again he was thinking not of her but of Harry.

It's convenience, she reminded herself for the thousandth time, but the reminder did little more than intensify the ache that had taken up residence in the region of her heart.

'Thanks, but, no, thanks,' she said, then thought back through his words to something that had caught her attention momentarily.

'You hired a car? You could have taken mine.'

Had it been yesterday or the day before, he'd proudly announced he'd fitted the baby capsule and returned her car to the private car park on the terrace?

'I didn't think of it.'

The words came out slowly, and he studied her intently, then took her in his arms again.

'We're strangers, aren't we?' he said softly, pressing his head against the top of hers so the words were filtered through her hair. 'With all the awkwardness that that entails.'

He hugged her tightly then released her to hold her where he could see her face again.

'It means we have to talk more to each other, until we learn to read each other's moods and know each other's secret doubts and fears. I've upset you, I know that, but I don't know why. All I can say, Joey, is that I'd never knowingly hurt you, and I hope to heaven that I won't do it unknowingly too often.'

Heaven help me, Joey thought, hugging him in turn. *How could I* not *have fallen in love with this man?*

Which didn't help all the nagging worries she had one bit!

He left the hospital and, knowing she'd not see him for the rest of the day, Joey decided it was time to think.

Really think, not get all muddled as she had the last time she'd considered the immediate future.

She had to work out, calmly and logically, just how they were going to go about this strange arrangement they had made.

What did it mean in practical terms?

First things first. Harry was due to come out of hospital any day now—would Max expect to move in?

Did he *want* to move in?

Did *she* want Max moving in?

And if he *did* move in, would the fact that he wouldn't always be there make things better or worse?

The shiver that went through her body could have been telling her she did want him to move in, for more than simple convenience. But it could equally have been apprehension. Could she live with this man she loved in the 'just good friends' way a convenient marriage seemed to dictate?

Except surely they'd got past that, discussing sex as part of the convenience?

She sighed and shut her eyes then opened them and looked up at the ceiling.

Nothing helped so she was actually pleased when there was a tap on the door and a nurse appeared, followed by another nurse wheeling a crib.

Harry's crib!

'Okay, Mum, are you ready for this?' the first one asked, and Joey forgot everything in the overwhelming rush of joy that, finally, she was going to be looking after her baby.

Just her!

Well, just her right now. For today, at least.

'Of course I am,' she said, and waited until the nurse had wheeled the crib in beside the bed and set it securely in place.

Joey lifted out the little boy, his eyes wide as he took in new surroundings. His head turned, then he focussed on her face, which she knew wasn't much more than a white blob to him right now.

But she was his white blob, and he seemed to know it, for he snuggled into her and her heart swelled with such love she thought it might explode.

'Ring if you need anything and don't forget he needs his sleep,' the older nurse reminded her, then the pair departed and Joey was alone with her son.

She knew tears were dribbling down her cheeks, and the tears reminded her of Max, who'd always seemed to be about to mop them up for her. She, who was *never* teary, had been like a waterspout here in the hospital.

'Your daddy should be here,' she told Harry, setting him down on the bed so she could examine him from top to toe, feeling him, touching him, finally believing he was truly hers.

And Max's, because she knew his love was just as great—his love for Harry, that was.

He slept in his crib beside the bed, Joey unable to take her eyes off him. He woke and fed, and she changed and talked to him, feeling the intensity of his regard, aware that right from the moment he'd been born he'd been taking in the big wide world around him, learning all the time.

It was late afternoon when the visitors arrived, barely making the visiting hours the hospital adhered to fairly strictly.

And after the euphoria of the day with her son, their arrival was so startling, shocking even, Joey couldn't move, couldn't speak.

Not that her silence was even noticed by David's mother, Marion, who was drawn to the crib the moment she entered the room.

While Paul, David's father, greeted Joey with a gentle kiss and deposited an armload of gifts on the bed, Marion was bending over the crib, peering at Harry, the smile on her face so vibrant, so alive with love and delight Joey knew she'd never be able to tell her.

Never!

'He's awake! Can I hold him?' Marion looked up at Joey, who had to laugh when she caught the expression of guilt that flashed across her visitor's face. 'Oh, Joey,' she continued, 'I didn't even say hello. How are you? Are you well? Is everything all right? The operation? Your email said it went well?'

'Of course you can hold him, and everything's fine with Harry and with me,' Joey replied.

Mostly!

She watched as Marion lifted Harry, holding him as if he was the most precious thing on earth, peering down at him, studying him, finally lifting her head to look at Joey again.

'He's the spitting image of David when he was born,' she said, tears now streaking *her* cheeks. 'He got so fair later, David, but when he was born he was as dark as this, and look…'

She carried Harry closer, sitting down on the bed beside Joey and unwinding the top of the wrap that snuggled him up. 'See, it's the McMillan thistle! You'd remember David had it too. And Paul—show her, Paul.'

Joey's mind all but shut down.

Shock, disbelief and an overwhelming desire to yell or scream jostled in her mind, while her heart raced with a desperation she didn't fully understand.

But Marion was pointing to the faintest of marks that could, with a lot of imagination, have been the shape of a thistle, just behind Harry's left armpit.

Joey blinked. She'd bathed and changed Harry many times since he'd left the SCU, and not noticed it.

How could she *not* have noticed it?

And *not* been reminded that David had had just such a mark—very faint—in exactly the same place?

Because she'd been too busy thinking of Max instead of David?

Now guilt joined the mess of emotions rattling through her, so while Paul obligingly took off his shirt to show his birthmark and Marion clucked and fussed, instantly besotted over Harry, Joey sat in stunned bemusement, rather hoping it might all turn out to be a dream.

Marion was sitting in a chair now, Harry asleep in her arms, and Paul was explaining how they'd begun to make arrangements to return home as soon as they'd received Joey's email about the baby's early arrival.

'Marion wouldn't have seen anything of Ireland if she'd stayed,' he said. 'Her mind was totally focussed on getting home, although it wasn't all that easy to arrange because we were on this tour with group bookings and all.'

'It was so good of you to come,' Joey managed to say, although she was still finding it difficult to think, let alone speak. 'You'll stay for a while. I can give you the keys to the flat, although I left in such a hurry it could be in a mess.'

Paul shook his head.

'We're booked back to Melbourne on an evening flight. There's another complication, something we didn't want to tell you while you were pregnant. We took the trip because Marion's not well. She's got cancer. She's had treatment, and was in remission—but…'

Now tears were welling in *his* eyes and Joey left the bed to give him a hug.

'She can have more treatment,' Paul explained, 'but now we're home, the sooner they start it the better.'

Joey felt her own tears returning and swallowed hard. She looked across at Marion, whose eyes were feasting on the baby in her arms, and saw the slightly sallow skin, the loss of weight.

'Come up whenever you can, and I'll come down to you if you'll have us both,' Joey said to Paul. 'Once I've got Harry into a routine, I'll be happy to travel with him.'

Paul hugged her and they sat a while in silence, until Marion stood up, gently settled Harry in his crib, then crossed to Joey, hugging her hard.

'Thank you,' she said, and the simple, oft-used words almost broke Joey's heart.

They left as suddenly as they'd arrived, insisting Joey stay in her room with Harry rather than seeing them even as far as the elevator.

'We'll be back,' Marion said. 'Now I've got a grandson to love, I refuse to let that cancer beat me.'

Joey collapsed on the bed and studied the ceiling—again! No answers written there, but now the reality of what had happened—the clinic, despite all their assurances, had made not one but two mistakes—was sinking in and, rising from the mess, a tall, lanky figure with unruly hair and green eyes…

Max loved Harry as much as she did, and now she'd have to tell him.

Tell him what?

Harry wasn't his child?

They'd have to do a DNA test, but the thistle birthmark surely told the truth...

She lifted the phone and asked the nurse at the desk to put her through to Bob Jenkins. By now he knew the whole story of the muddled IVF—or of what they'd thought was the whole story. She could talk to him about it.

Get him to tell Max?

'Of course not, you wuss,' she was muttering to herself when Bob picked up.

'Are you calling me a wuss?' he demanded.

'Not you, me,' she told him. 'Are you at the hospital?'

'Just leaving,' he said.

'Could I ask a favour?'

Bob agreed he'd come straight to her room, and by the time he arrived she'd calmed down enough to be able to explain what had happened and ask him to do a DNA test on Harry for her.

'Max isn't going to like this,' he said, adding to the already unbearable load of anxiety Joey was feeling.

'I can't help that, I just need to know,' she snapped. 'You're Harry's doctor, not Max's friend right now, so will you do it? And rush it through if you can?'

'You know it'll take three to five days for a familial test even if I rush it, and you'll need a sample from Max as well.'

Joey flopped back onto the bed.

'Of course I will. I hadn't thought of that. Let it go for now, Bob. I'm sorry to have held you up.'

'No worries,' he said, and turned towards the door. Joey stood up to say goodbye, and he turned and gave her a hug.

'Call me if you need me for anything at all,' he said. Then he kissed her cheek and added, 'You'll work it out'

As if!

How could she possibly work it out?

And what of Max?

Just how hurt was he going to be, learning Harry wasn't his child?

Max had held him, sat with him through the long nights, chatting to him, singing silly songs—Joey had crept in one night and heard him—fed him and even bathed him.

Max loved him.

But he had to know!

Or did he?

Didn't he argue about truth at all costs?

Oh, hell!

There was no way she couldn't tell, because not telling would tie Max to her through a lie and what sort of a basis for a relationship would that be?

Joey looked at the ring that had been on her finger for such a short time and sighed, and she felt like little bits of her so recently mended heart were breaking off.

The meeting with the dean had taken longer than Max expected, so it was dark as he headed back towards the city. Joey's text, early in the day, had told him Harry was rooming in with her, preparatory to them both going home.

It had been okay at the hospital where, as Harry's father, he'd had equal access to his child, but home?

Somehow he was engaged to a woman he barely knew, with a son he hadn't ever expected to have, and a future with the two of them that was a complete blank.

Though an exciting blank, he was sure.

Somehow, intent on getting Harry through the first few weeks of his life, the subject of what happened next hadn't been discussed.

Did a convenient marriage mean they'd live together?

His body wanted this and from the kisses they'd shared he was fairly certain Joey's body wanted it as well.

But was that enough?

And if they did live together, then where?

Joey's apartment was close to her work—convenient for her—and he had no fixed abode, although if he agreed to the Sunshine Coast research base after he returned from Africa, he'd be working two hours north of the city. A long commute.

Driving gave you too much time to think, he decided. But his mind kept going round in circles, question after question, and no answers anywhere, because although they'd kissed and agreed to parental responsibilities, beyond that the future remained blank.

Hugely, frighteningly blank.

We'll work it out, he told himself, but even to himself it didn't sound convincing.

He drove straight to the hospital, although it was well after visiting hours. He assumed Joey would be asleep, but after the agonising uncertainty of the drive, he had to see her.

Had to see Harry too, but this time it was Joey he really needed to see.

She *was* asleep.

As was Harry, nestled in his wrappings in the crib beside her bed.

One of Joey's hands rested on the edge of the crib, the other lay on top of the sheet that covered her.

The sight of them, both ringless, struck panic into Max's heart, although when he saw the little ring box on the shelf beside the bed, he kind of settled down.

Perhaps some women didn't wear their rings to bed.

Or perhaps Joey was just afraid of wearing it while feeding Harry, afraid she might scratch him.

Max sank into the one comfortable chair hospitals seemed to allow to each room and tried to still his still irregular heartbeats.

There'd be an explanation.

Something so simple he'd feel stupid.

He reminded himself that this was his family, right here in this room with him, and closed his eyes.

Harry's cry was muted, almost apologetic, but Joey was attuned to it. She eased herself up on the bed, bent over the crib and lifted out the still tiny baby.

Change him first so he can go back into his crib if he falls asleep while feeding, she reminded herself.

Everything was to hand, and it took only seconds to get him dry and comfortable. He was more insistent now, although still quiet in his grizzling as he nuzzled at her chest in search of food.

'Hey, you, be patient,' she said, then she smiled as he found her nipple and began to suckle, his eyes wide, fixed on her face, telling her all kinds of things she knew were mostly love.

It was only when she reached out on the other side of the bed to find another pillow to prop behind her back that she noticed Max, sleeping quietly in the chair in the darker corner of the room.

'Max!'

She barely breathed the word, but his eyes opened and, seeing her there, the baby at her breast, he smiled.

And more bits broke away from her heart.

'We have to talk,' she said, speaking softly so as not to disturb Harry's feed.

'Now?'

He made the word sound incredulous, as if it was the last thing they should be doing in the middle of the night.

'I think so,' she said, 'and I don't know how to say this. There's no easy way. We're kind of back where you first burst into my life, so I guess I do as I suggested you do then and just spit it out.'

Her heart was faltering, her pulse fluttering and she was struggling to keep breathing, but it had to be said because prolonging what would be a deception was unthinkable.

'David's parents were here today. They both agreed he's the spitting image of David as a newborn and there's more—the thistle.'

'What the hell has a thistle to do with *my* child?'

The words came out as a muted roar, and Max congratulated himself that he'd kept it muted. Somehow, some way he sensed what was coming and he wanted to rage against the entire world—and very loudly.

He did not want to hear this.

Maybe he had to.

'I'll explain,' Joey was saying, moving Harry from one breast to the other, 'when he's finished. And I know we'll have to do DNA tests on him and on you, and I spoke to Bob today—'

'You told Bob this before you told me?'

Less muted now but how was he expected to feel, to handle this betrayal?

'I wanted to ask him how long the test would take. He didn't take a sample from Harry, I wouldn't let him do that until I'd spoken to you, but if the clinic made one mistake it could just as easily have made two. And it's three to five days for familial testing, but as you're due to go to Africa… I'm sorry…'

She'd rushed her explanation—getting all the devastation slammed down on his head at once, but her voice had trailed away at the end and he guessed telling him this had been as hard for her as it had been for him to listen.

Except she got to keep the child!

Anger vied with pain inside his chest, and he struck out at her.

'So the ring's back in its box? You're returning it? No convenient marriage after all! You must be relieved.'

He might as well have slapped her across the cheek, the way she flinched and from the pain he read too clearly on her face.

But she pulled herself together—she was made of steel, this woman.

'If you think that you didn't know me very well,' she said. 'So perhaps...' She took a deep breath and he saw the pain wash over her face. But when she spoke the resolution was back. 'Perhaps I should be relieved.'

She reached across and picked up the ring from the bed-side table, passing it to him.

'Harry's finished now. I'll show you.'

She put him down on the bed between them and un-swaddled him, turning him gently on his side, lifting the little shirt he was wearing to reveal a very faint but distinctive birthmark.

Definitely a thistle!

'I hadn't noticed, hadn't given it a thought,' she was saying, 'but David had it in the same place and his father, Paul, showed me his today. I don't think it's coincidence, Max, although of course we should have the tests.'

He could tell she was hurting, but what did she know of hurt? This revelation—even before the bloody thistle show—had been like a punch in his gut. He could barely breathe, let alone think.

Harry wasn't *his*?

This little sprog he'd sat with, held, bathed and fed wasn't his?

But he'd delivered him, helped to name him, taken him wholly and completely into his heart.

He *had* to get away, had to leave before he betrayed himself in some way—yelling, screaming out the anguish deep inside him, or, even worse, howling like a madman, howling with grief for his son.

'I'll be going, then,' he said, and he pocketed the ring.

And he walked straight out. He almost ran.

He left the room, leaving Joey sitting on the bed, Harry sleeping in her arms, pain and blood seeping from her shattered heart.

CHAPTER THIRTEEN

THE SETTLEMENT IN Zambia showed Harry the human face of the AIDS epidemic, the number of orphans there unimaginable to Western minds. He was collecting statistics, assessing the success of earlier education programmes and also assisting with the anti-malarial steps the community was taking. His work kept him fully occupied.

Almost fully occupied.

A young woman with a baby strapped to her breast could send his heart into overdrive and plunge his mind into gloom, but he kept going, determined to do whatever he could to help the smiling, gentle people among whom he worked.

The medical team was accommodated in Lusaka, not far from the village where they were concentrating their energies, but Harry chafed against the time it took to travel to and from their makeshift clinic and research centre. The separation from the locals made them more outsiders.

'I'm sure we'd get more people taking part in our programmes if we were closer to them,' he argued with the team leader.

'By living out there? You have *got* to be joking!'

'But there are other aid workers living in the settlement,' he pointed out. 'Anyway, I'd like to do it. I can find somewhere to stay.'

'It's no skin off my nose,' the leader told him. 'Do what

you want, only don't kill yourself in the process. You're already working twice as hard as anyone else on the team, helping out in the village.'

Because I need to be exhausted before I can sleep, Max could have explained, but didn't. He'd found that only by working all the hours he could was he able to, for a while, put Joey and Harry out of his mind.

Most of the time!

So he shifted into the village, sharing a patched-up hut with a volunteer from America, who was helping dig new wells as the older ones had become polluted.

Digging, Max found, when he offered to help after his day's work was finished, was a very satisfactory way of exhausting himself, although his new American friend suspected something was amiss, asking questions about Harry's life back home.

'I have no life,' Harry snapped, rolling over so his back was to his friend.

But the words echoed around the room, and the defeat he heard in them shocked him to the core.

When had *he* ever been defeated?

Sleep didn't come. He woke and went back to work. At midday he paused to watch a girl walking along the dusty track to the central well. She had a toddler in her arms, and a little girl was clinging to her hip.

She was surely too young to be their mother? And how could she possibly carry water?

But as he watched, a man came up behind her. Gnarled and stooped with age.

The little girl left the older girl's side and greeted him with delight.

He had pots. He and the girl did the filling, then both of them, teenager and grandfather, walked slowly back along the track.

To home?

They were a family. He knew it with a certainty he didn't

understand. Grandfather, granddaughter, nieces, nephews or younger siblings? Whoever was left in this AIDS-ravaged district.

And he'd walked away from Joey and Harry.

Why? Because he was afraid to love? Because he didn't know how to love?

He did. He watched the retreating group and thought it was as hard and as easy as that.

Throw your heart in the ring and love.

If he hadn't messed it up forever.

Joey gave the window she was cleaning a final rub, put down her cloth and looked at her watch, wondering when Harry would wake up for another feed.

And a bath, and maybe a walk in the park across the road!

The awareness that she was wishing her life away struck her like a physical blow. Was it the fact that she'd cleaned the same window two days ago that had made her realise just how pointless her life had become?

Not pointless as far as she and Harry were concerned, but he was practically the perfect baby, eating and sleeping—sleeping longer and longer between feeds—and once she'd put the washing on, fed herself and Harry, swept the floor and fluffed the cushions, she would find herself at a loss as to what to do.

She had a locum doing her work for six months, after which she'd intended to return to work part-time, taking Harry with her, with a nanny doing a few hours a day to entertain him when she couldn't.

Now, she realised, this was when she should be working, while all he did was sleep and eat.

How could she, a paediatrician, not have known something so fundamental?

Because she'd never had a baby?

Although not all of them were as placid as Harry.

She sighed.

Used to being organised, the daily tasks of housekeeping were a simple routine, done within an hour at the most, which left an awful lot of the day to be filled in.

Max would have filled them in!

He wouldn't have had to be there with her, but thinking about him, deciding what to cook for dinner, shopping for things he might like to eat...

The realisation that she didn't really know what he liked to eat—apart from big breakfasts and T-bone steak—sent a spurt of sadness through her body.

One more spurt to join all the others. Sadness was dogging her heels every day.

If Max were here, she could redecorate the apartment—buy a new bed, new bed linen—take Harry to the shops and go crazy.

Can't you do that anyway? the sane voice in her head enquired.

But there was no impetus to do it—no one to say, yes, that would be great, or, no, I don't like bright blue.

For the first time in all the years since David had died she realised just how hard it was to be alone, to have no one there to share today and tomorrow—all the tomorrows.

No one to learn to know. To find out why he hated bright blue.

And she felt like weeping.

The programme ended, and although Harry would have liked to stay on digging wells for a little longer, he had to get home.

Home to Harry and, more importantly, home to Harry's mother. For the more he thought about it, the more certain he'd become.

She'd handed back his ring as if the only connection between them had been a tiny baby they both happened to love.

For the time in Africa had cemented things in his mind. He'd watched kids looking after kids, extended families, women taking children whose parents had died from AIDS. He'd watched the love shared, growing, expanding to encompass all comers.

And things had settled in his heart. Forget the DNA. Harry was more his than any other man's, although, in a way, he was glad for Joey's sake, and for David's parents, that he had David's DNA.

But Harry was his, that much he knew.

And so was Joey.

He kept seeing the little family, grandfather and kids, and he thought it wasn't just about care of the little ones. He saw the deep affection between them.

He knew without being told that their lives had been shattered, yet they were open to love again, in whatever guise it took.

If not love, what was there? A great gaping void. A void he no longer had room for.

So now...now all he had to do was convince Harry's mother of the fact and sort out a few things. Like when they could get married and where they'd live. If she'd have him.

The university had a lovely apartment for him up at the coast—high on a hill looking out over the ocean. Joey was on maternity leave, she might as well be near the beach...

His heart crunched into a tight ball just thinking of her—just thinking that he might have lost her.

Joey heard the argument being conducted on the stairs right through her reasonably heavy door.

One voice, the shrill one, belonged to Jean, her neighbour on the floor below, and the self-appointed ruler of the building.

'You had no right to just walk in behind me,' she was saying. 'Go back down and ring the bell of Joanne's apartment the way you're supposed to do. Then she'll ask you who you are and let you in if she wants you in.'

The other voice was softer, less distinct, definitely male and hauntingly familiar.

Max?

It couldn't be!

Max here?

The voices were growing louder, Jean's more strident, the male voice more insistent.

'I'm telling you—' from Jean.

Would he push her down the stairs? Would she push him?

Joey could stand it no longer. She opened the door and peered down to the landing below where the argument was taking place.

'Tell him what, Jean?' she asked.

'That you might not want to see him. He followed me in, Joanne. I didn't realise it until he caught up on the landing.'

But Joey was beyond responding, beyond words, for it was Max looking up at her, a Max she barely recognised as uncertainty had blurred his features.

But only for an instant, for now he was coming up towards her, two steps at a time, Jean still bleating protests as he reached the top and took Joey in his arms.

'I love you,' he said, loudly enough for the whole building to hear. 'I realised I hadn't said it, or maybe I didn't know it then and needed to have you taken from me to realise it. But I do love you, Joey, and Harry too, because Harry's mine, you know that, it's the bonding thing you spoke of. We've bonded. We're family, Joey.'

She was as gobsmacked as she assumed Jean, still hovering below, must be, but as Joey looked into Max's face, so close to hers, so familiar, so loved, she saw that terrible uncertainty creeping back into it and knew she couldn't have that.

'And I love you,' she whispered, and kissed him on the lips.

Hunger flared between them, the kiss deepening until every cell in her body trembled with desire, and it was all she could do to get both of them inside the door before she ran her hands across his body, feeling him, remembering him, ready to strip away his clothes so they could learn each other completely for the very first time.

A little bleat from a bedroom—

'The master's voice?' Max said, his voice so husky she knew his hunger was as desperate as her own.

'Of course,' Joey muttered, 'and it's bathtime as well. Then, wouldn't you know it, this is the time of the day when he stays awake for an hour or so, expecting to be entertained.'

Max hugged her close.

'I think we can wait an hour or two,' he said, nuzzling a kiss against her neck. 'After all, we've got a lifetime of loving ahead of us, my darling.'

And as Joey broke away she felt her heart swell, all the pieces back in place.

'He's in the back bedroom, he'll be pleased to see you,' she told Max, who looked at her, uncertain again.

'Of course he's yours,' she told him. 'He's been asking for you every day.'

She followed Max into Harry's room and saw the love radiating from Max's face as he bent over the bassinet.

'Hi, little man,' he said softly, and Harry smiled his first smile—his very first—and as he hadn't been fed, it couldn't possibly be wind.

Max picked him up and changed him, then carried him into the living room, handing him to Joey, who was tugging open her bra.

Then he sat on the arm of the big chair and watched them both—his family—and talked of Africa, of missing them and that learning love was essential for his life. Love and a family to love.

And Joey told him how she'd missed him, how the long empty days had dragged without him—without even allowing herself to think about him, assuming he was gone forever.

'I could have to go away again,' Max reminded her, and she smiled at him over their baby's head.

'But you'll be with me in my thoughts, with us both, because you're in our hearts and we're in yours so we'll never really be separated.'

Grown men didn't cry, especially strong men who climbed great mountains and went on rescue missions. So Max dug in his pocket and found the ring, and through only slightly blurry eyes slipped it onto Joey's finger. Then he kissed her on the top of her head and touched Harry's cheek and said thank you to the fates for giving him such joy.

EPILOGUE

MAX HAD BEEN up for hours, hanging balloons and streamers in the big fig tree in the park across the road from the apartment, marking out the area for their party.

From the bedroom window, Joey could see the results of his labour, and she lifted Harry, who was zooming a small car around her feet, so he could share the view.

His smile, though, was not for balloons or streamers but for his father, who was crossing the road on his way back to the apartment.

'Dada,' Harry cried, patting his hand against the glass.

'Yes, Dada will be home soon,' Joey assured him, setting him back on the floor and stretching her already aching muscles in her back.

This second baby—this unexpected gift because they'd not known if Max could father a child—had been more difficult to carry, awake and kicking when Joey wanted to sleep, pressing a foot hard on its mother's bladder when she was seeing a patient.

They'd both decided they didn't want to know the sex, and now the birth was imminent Joey found herself arguing for both—wouldn't a girl be fun, but a brother for Harry would be great as well.

'In the meantime, young man,' she said as she moved a small car from under her foot, 'we have your birthday party. Grandad and Grandma will be here, and Aunty Lissa and

Kirstie, and Nana Winthrop with a whole hoard of assorted Winthrop aunts, uncles and cousins. Your father should have chartered a plane to bring them down.'

For Max's predictions had been right. His family had showered Harry with gifts and affection, enclosing Joey in the love they had for each other, giving her a wider family than she and Max and Harry. They came and went, always calling in if they were in town, often coming especially to see them. In fact, it was Max's mum, Linda, who would stay on so there'd be someone here for Harry when Joey went to hospital for this baby, and one of Max's nieces did the nanny work, minding Harry when Joey returned to work part-time.

'A family too big for you ever to be alone again,' Max had said to her when they'd travelled north to be married in his home town.

And as Joey had got to know them, she'd realised how true the words had been, for she'd been enfolded in their love, become one of them.

She'd never be alone again.

'Dada!' Harry yelled, and Joey knew Max must be on the stairs, for Harry always heard his tread before she did.

She lifted her son and went to the door, wanting to open it to him on this special day, the anniversary of their son's birth but special for the two of them as well, for it was twelve months since the strangest of mistakes and coincidences had brought her and Max together, twelve months since her journey into love had begun.

'Love you,' Max said, kissing Harry on the head before lifting him onto his hip.

'And you,' he said to Joey, drawing her close, holding her tightly, breathing kisses on her head. 'More than words can ever say,' he added quietly.

She looked up at him and saw the words echoed in his eyes—a look of such overwhelming love she felt her bones melt and wondered if she'd ever stop melting when Max looked at her, or held her, or told her that he loved her.

'Love you, too,' she whispered, and reached up, awkwardly, to kiss him on the lips.

* * * * *

A sneaky peek at next month...

MEDICAL
ROMANCE

THE ULTIMATE IN ROMANTIC MEDICAL DRAMA

My wish list for next month's titles...

In stores from 1st August 2014:

❏ Tempted by Her Boss – Scarlet Wilson

& His Girl From Nowhere – Tina Beckett

❏ Falling For Dr Dimitriou – Anne Fraser

& Return of Dr Irresistible – Amalie Berlin

❏ Daring to Date Her Boss – Joanna Neil

& A Doctor to Heal Her Heart – Annie Claydon

Available at WHSmith, Tesco, Asda, Eason, Amazon and Apple

Just can't wait?

Special Offers

Every month we put together collections and longer reads written by your favourite authors.

Here are some of next month's highlights— and don't miss our fabulous discount online!

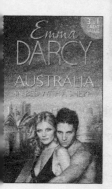

On sale 18th July

On sale 18th July

On sale 18th July

Ex&P

Join our *EXCLUSIVE* eBook club

FROM JUST £1.99 A MONTH!

Never miss a book again with our hassle-free eBook subscription.

★ Pick how many titles you want from each series with our flexible subscription

★ Your titles are delivered to your device on the first of every month

★ Zero risk, zero obligation!

There really is nothing standing in the way of you and your favourite books!

Start your eBook subscription today at www.millsandboon.co.uk/subscribe